A FEW FAIR DAYS

For Jane Gardam the best sound in the world is "a child laughing out loud at a book", and her first books – *A Few Fair Days*, *A Long Way from Verona* and *Bilgewater* – have been making children laugh for nearly twenty years. Her fourth book, *God on the Rocks*, was runner up for the Booker Prize and *The Hollow Land* was serialised on television and won the Whitbread Award for Children's Fiction. Her other titles include *The Summer After the Funeral*, *Through the Dolls' House Door* (now a Walker Books paperback) and several shorter books for younger children – one of which, *Bridget and William*, was commended for the Carnegie Medal.

Like Lucy, the small girl who is the central character of *A Few Fair Days*, Jane Gardam was born and brought up on the north east coast of Yorkshire – and also like Lucy, she had several interesting aunts. She still has a home in Yorkshire, as well as an old house in Kent which has the ruins of a monastery, a chapel and a ghost in the garden.

Jane Gardam is married to an international lawyer, with whom she has travelled all over the world – from Java to Jamaica. She has three children, one of whom, her daughter Catharine, is the author and illustrator of two children's picture books.

Also by Jane Gardam

JANE GARDAM

A Few Fair Days

Gabriel

with lo

f

Gg

WALKER BOOKS
LONDON

FOR DAVID

First published 1971 by Hamish Hamilton Ltd
New edition first published 1987 by Julia MacRae Books
This edition published 1989 by Walker Books Ltd
87 Vauxhall Walk, London SE11 5HJ

Text © 1971, 1987 Jane Gardam
Cover illustration © 1987 Anthony Browne

Printed in Great Britain by Cox & Wyman Ltd, Reading
Typeset by Computape (Pickering) Ltd

British Library Cataloguing in Publication Data
Gardam, Jane
A few fair days.
I. Title
823'.914[J]   PZ7
ISBN 0-7445-1337-5

'And shall I ask at the day's end once more
What beauty is, and what I can have meant
By happiness?'

EDWARD THOMAS

Contents

1

The Wonderful Day

It began badly. Grand aunts were coming to tea and nobody wanted Lucy. "What shall I *do*?" she asked her mother who was finishing cakes. "Help me, dear," said her mother slapping and beating in a cloud of flour. "But I can't," said Lucy.

This was true. A tea party for special visitors was a very complicated affair indeed. It was expert work and Lucy was right. She couldn't help, except to carry things through to the table at twenty-five past three, and be polite and quiet when everything began.

Lucy lived not so many years ago in a small cold town by the sea in the farthest part of the north of Yorkshire where things changed very slowly. For a long, long time in this town, tea parties had meant

> one fruit cake
> one sponge cake (chocolate)
> one plate of small iced cakes
> scones with currants
> scones without currants
> one of Auntie Bea's tea-cakes
> one of Jinnie Love's Fair Days
> drop scones (or dropped scoanes)
> home-made jam
> heather honey

very thin slices of white bread and butter
very thin slices of brown bread and butter
a Sad Mary
brandy snaps with cream
spirit kettle newly polished
spidery cloth that gets in your feet.

All the things have to be freshly made on the day of the party, except for the fruit cake which has to be kept for a month before in an old black biscuit tin with an apple in it. A good smell of sea-captains comes out when you take off the lid.

Of course some people will tell you that in Yorkshire you have ham and salad and tinned peaches for tea, but this is not true if aunts are coming. Not true at all. It has been buns and bits since the Vikings.

So – her mother was very busy and Lucy was in the way and went to look for her father. She found him in the greenhouse smartening up his chrysanthemums ready to show the grand aunts. There were dozens of tall flowers standing to attention on the benches in large pots.

They made a forest of black, ragged leaves draggling out of bony trunks, and far above Lucy's head she could see theirs like pretty curly mops – white and bright yellow and sugar-pink and dark red with yellow underneaths.

"What can I *do*?" asked Lucy.

"What can you do?" said her father, nipping off a leaf.

"What can you do?" He shuffled the pots about and gazed at the flowers in a dream. "Seven sevens?" he suddenly shouted out. So Lucy went away. (Her father was a schoolmaster.)

She went into the dining-room where Phyllis the maid was polishing the table as if her life depended upon it. She was all skin and bone and had a wild old face and crashed about the furniture muttering to herself. Lucy wasn't frightened of her because she had known her all her life, but anyone else would have been frightened to death. "What can I *do*?" Phyllis rolled her mad red eyes around in her head and screamed, "Git owt of tway. I'll nivver be done. Git owt an nivver bother me."

So Lucy went out. She hadn't ever gone out alone before – but now it seemed the right thing to do. She walked down the path, out of the gate, down the lane, across the main road and onto the promenade which went curving round for a long way with tall Victorian houses on one side, called pretty names like 'Sans Souci' and 'North Winds', and a stony slope to the sea-shore on the other. Now and again in the stony slope there was a smooth run-down for fishing boats and down one of these went Lucy.

She was joined by a dog. He came bounding up to her all covered in sand and very wet. He had long orange hair, and was almost as big as she was. Together they set off along the sands towards the breakwater.

It was a lovely day, very sunny and a bit cold. Not too

cold to paddle, however, and Lucy took off her shoes and
socks and went in up to her knees, sucking in her teeth a
bit. The sand was lovely and clean and gritty under her
feet and there were patches of shiny sea-coal. The dog
came in, too, and danced in the sea and tried to gallop and
to leap right out of it. Once he nearly knocked Lucy over.
Then a wave came and went rather high and she found
that even her hair was wet.

So she decided to run about and get warm and the dog
did, too. They raced all over the great empty beach until
they both fell down snorting and panting in a patch of
glittering black sea-coal.

As they sat, an old woman, wearing a man's cap back
to front, came pushing a little cart out of the sandhills.
She had only one eye and her face was very dirty. She
came and sat next to Lucy and the dog in the sea-coal,
and taking a little tin from inside her jacket she opened it
and began to chew a strip of shiny black bending stuff.
She offered a bit to Lucy but Lucy didn't take it.

"What's that?" she asked.

"It's baccy," said the queer woman. "What're you
doin 'ere all by yerselluf?"

"I'm not by myself," said Lucy, and the dog came and
sat in between them and looked hard at the woman.

"Most chiller's afeared o' me," said the woman. "They
sez I'se mad, and me Gran were a smuggler."

"Phyllis's Gran was a smuggler, too," said Lucy. "She
looks mad but she's not really."

6

"My great grandad found a corpse on these sands – a dead, dead sailor. And this sailor had a ring on his finger and my great grandad he cut this ring off, ant finger too," said the old woman. "But 'e 'ad no luck after." She spat the tobacco out of her mouth and got up and began to shovel the sea-coal into the cart.

"I could carry yer off wi' me," she said. The dog growled. "But I nivver would. 'Ere," she said, "gis yer 'ands. 'Old 'em up in a basket." Lucy held up her hands and the woman dropped about a dozen little round shells into them, as small as a baby's first tooth. They shone in the sun. "Them's nanny-nuns, the luckiest things in the world," she said. "Care for them kindly."

Lucy walked on with the dog behind her. After a long time the shadows changed and didn't follow her any more. A long time again and she reached the breakwater and watched the green sea curling in, and the coloured seaweed and the far-away smoke from the chimneys of the steel works colouring the sky red and yellow and cream, and the big ships sliding by in the distance to lie among the crooked cranes in the dockyard. The sea sighed, and slept and sighed again.

She didn't want to go home, but after a while she found herself turning and walking back over the sandhills. She pushed her feet into the white sand which began to flow down behind her in small waterfalls and then she went rolling down the other side, and the dog rolled, too. When they reached the golf course the dog began to tear round in circles with a grin on his face. Then he leapt up at her and licked her and suddenly was gone.

Lucy plodded on over a patch of round, neat, pale yellow turf with a flag and a ball on it. Far away a man shouted and seemed to be waving a stick, but she took no notice and climbed the stile into the churchyard. There still seemed to be nobody much about. In the church porch she heard a twittering and three fat young swallows looked down out of a little mud nest – six black eyes gleaming. She opened the church door and walked all round the church once. It was very quiet and the sun shone through the coloured glass in soft blobs on the stone aisles. Lucy sat down in a patch of it. Her feet were red, her legs were purple, her dress was green and her hands were blue. Then she walked up to the altar and looked at the lamb made out of gold stitches, carrying a little flag over its shoulder like the one on the golf course. When she turned round she could see her wet footmarks marching all round the church in a procession.

She came out on the other side of the churchyard and there was the meadow with the long grass waving and beyond that the railway line. All you had to do was to walk a little way beside the railway line and you came to the end of the road where her house was. She had been in a great circle and her legs quite ached. Her wet dress was sticking all over her and her wet hair was sticking to her head and she hadn't been able to get her socks on to her wet feet. She was very cold. Looking down at herself there seemed to be a great deal of sand and sea-coal sticking to her. Suddenly it felt queer and late.

Three old ladies were sitting on a green seat outside the meadow gate. They were very small old ladies with white hair, little button boots and high round collars like soldiers, but with little frills around the top. They all wore very high hats with veils. One had a gold watch round her neck on a chain, one had a brooch with a stone face on it, and one was holding a round bunch of red roses. They all nodded and smiled at Lucy and they looked so very old and queer and small that she thought, I suppose this is a dream, or I'm dead or something.

"What's this?" said one of them with a glint in her eye.

"I think it is a girl," said the second.

"It is a very wet girl," said the third, "and what is she holding in her hands?"

They nodded and smiled and nodded and smiled.

"Good angels," Lucy decided, and she said, "These are my shoes and socks in this hand because my feet are so wet, and they're nanny-nuns in the other."

"Nanny-nuns!" cried all three together. "Why, they are the luckiest things in the world!"

"An old woman without an eye whose grandad cut a ring off a dead sailor gave them to me," said Lucy. "On the beach."

"Aren't you rather – er – young-ish to be out alone?" asked the one with the roses. "Where do you live?"

Lucy didn't answer her for a moment. She thought

about home. "I think I'll be going now," she said gravely. "It's not far down the road."

"We are going down the road," said the old ladies, "to have tea with our great-niece. We were a little early so we came and sat in the meadow."

So Lucy and the grand aunts came home together and found as they turned the last corner that the whole world seemed to be gathered on the pavement, their arms in all directions. Lucy's mother was pulling on her gloves to go for the Vicar, her father was mounting his bicycle to go for the police and Phyllis was in tears.

But the grand aunts soon made everything quite all right, although Lucy had to promise not to go off alone again – not for years. She had a hot bath and came down to tea in a new print dress looking very pink, and ate and listened and beamed. And her mother ate and listened and beamed and the aunts ate and talked and beamed and her father told them many things about chrysanthemums and schoolmastering and Phyllis sang hymns in the kitchen, louder and louder as the afternoon came to an end. The tea was poured into the peacock cups and the jam shone in the glass dishes and the cakes and the scones and the brandy snaps were like flowers in a meadow.

"I don't know when we've *had* such a day!" said the grand aunts. They gave Lucy a very old needlebox when they left, with pale honeysuckle painted on it. She kept it on her bedroom mantelpiece with the nanny-nuns inside.

2

Auntie Kitty and the Fever House

As some children are born with a lot of hair or a lot of luck or a lot of spots or a lot of small knitted woolly jackets, Lucy was born with a lot of aunts. They came in all sizes – fat ones, thin ones, long ones, round ones, plump and pretty ones, queer old plain ones. There were great-aunts, great-great-aunts, step-aunts, real aunts, aunts-in-law and, thrown in for luck, various friends of her mother called 'courtesy aunts' to whom, Lucy thought for a long time, one ought to curtsey, though she didn't.

And then there was Auntie Kitty.

Now every aunt of Lucy's except for Auntie Kitty was quite certain about one thing: that it was right and proper to be born and grow up and die in the same place, especially if it happened to be on a five-mile stretch of the Yorkshire coast. If possible one should contrive to be born in one of two small towns, and preferably in a house looking over the cricket field. If one lived to ninety or so – as most of them did – there might be no harm in taking a little holiday now and then at Scarborough. But on the whole one kept to one's own fireside.

But Auntie Kitty! Auntie Kitty believed in the very opposite. She never, never stopped travelling. At the age of two she was brought back from the railway station under the station-master's arm – "Just sitting watching the trains, Ma'am. Good as gold." At the age of nine she

13

was away with a hat box and found with difficulty on the new trunk road to Middlesbrough, heading for the docks. At the age of nineteen, after learning rather fast to be a nurse, she was on an ocean liner, waving a silk handkerchief and smiling like an angel in heaven. And after that she was seldom seen again.

Perhaps once a year a very old-looking postcard would appear from Auntie Kitty with a picture of somewhere quite extraordinary and wonderful, and it would be passed round and someone would be sure to say, "Oh well – Kitty!" Once she sent Lucy a bag from South America made of skins and coloured beads, with a note saying, 'To be hung from the saddle.' Lucy had no saddle but she carried it about with her until the dog ate it and she found the pieces in his basket. Then she cried and carried on and her mother said, "What can I *do* with this child?"

Lucy liked to watch some of her other aunts dusting because of Auntie Kitty, for when the duster got near to Kitty's photograph on the piano – and a very pretty photograph it was, of a girl like a rose petal, with sloping shoulders and drooping eyelashes, and a bunch of forget-me-nots pinned into a lovely lace dress – they would start flicking in a different way, as if they wouldn't mind too much if a corner went into Kitty's eye. "The Lady Kitty," Aunt Dolly said almost every time. Lucy studied the photograph very carefully.

Soon after Lucy's brother Jake was born, Lucy's

mother caught the scarlet fever and was driven away in an ambulance. The day she went off, Lucy was taken round to tea with two very old aunts called Fanny and Beatrice in their lovely airy house (overlooking the cricket field) where there was a cake-stand called 'The Curate's Aid', a silver muffin dish, a bright fire and old glass paperweights catching the light.

The two old ladies kept passing her things and looked very sad. Later on Lucy learned that most of her aunts took even the smallest illnesses very seriously because they had few other excitements, but she didn't understand this then. After tea they all walked round to visit another old lady, and sat in another drawing-room where they talked in low tones and looked at Lucy very sorrowfully and the new old lady creaked to her feet and came across the pink carpet very slowly to give Lucy a piece of sugared ginger which was beastly.

When she got home her father was pacing the sitting-room on his own with the door shut, the angry maid, Phyllis, was crashing about boiling up the baby bottles, and poor little Jake was howling his head off. Lucy sat by him as he was bathed.

"Jes' you wait an' see yon babby by 'is Mam's 'ome," said Phyllis, soaping away. "Alf starved 'e's bin. Jes' you wait."

"When will Mother come back?" asked Lucy.

"Nivver thee mind. Jes' give me time to put fat on yon babby."

15

"Where's Mother gone?"
"To't Fever 'Ouse, o' course."

Friday was visiting day. Father was being taken by a friend with a motor car to see Mother "through the window", and Lucy was to go with him for the ride. She sat alone in the back, low down in the leather, and watched the country go by. First there was the long straight road leading away from the sea, with thin trees on either side. The trees had turned their backs on the sea and their branches streamed out in front of them like hair in their eyes. There were cornfields and potato fields and beyond them on the right the chimneys and towers of the steel works like ships in the meadows. Then came a great house, a church, a row of cottages, a sharp bend and hills that climbed up to heather and sheep and dropped down to a big quiet village with a high street as wide as a field. On they went and at last began to climb up a long, wooded road and stopped beside iron railings, leathery laurel bushes with spots on and a high black door which said DO NOT OPEN THIS DOOR in big white letters.

What is the good of a door, thought Lucy, if you can't open it, but her father pulled a bell-pull and after a moment the door opened inwards and he disappeared.

Lucy sat and looked at the back of the driver, one of the new young masters at her father's school. He had big crooked ears loosely joined to his head and very bright, sandy hair. He stared straight ahead.

He stared straight ahead and Lucy stared straight ahead for about a hundred years. It was very hot in the car. The leather smelled of horses. Nobody passed by. Not a leaf moved. When at last her father came back everything took a deep breath and the birds began to sing.

This happened every Friday for four weeks. Once or twice the driver cleared his throat, but never did he speak or even turn round and look at Lucy. Once he took a bag of sweets out of the dashboard, carefully undid a toffee and put it in his mouth.

On the fifth Friday Lucy spoke. She said, all of a sudden in a queer deep voice that gave her a shock, "YOU HAVE GOT AWFUL EARS."

The man immediately fell out of the car in a heap and spent the rest of the long, long hour pacing about, proudly examining first the sky and then his shoes and clenching his teeth on his pipe. "Nice young fellow," her father said the next day at tea-time. "Pity he can't drive us again. He's taken on extra cricket practice. Says he can't stand cricket either. Hard-working chap."

The next week Lucy spent Friday afternoon with Aunt Jane, a beautiful, graceful aunt who took her for a walk on the golf links. "Look at all the bunny holes, Lucy dear. All the mummy bunnies are tying bibs on the baby bunnies and sitting them down to tea." She thinks I'm a baby, thought Lucy. She didn't mind at all.

But still nobody told her a thing about her mother. Her father never seemed to be about, Phyllis had fallen in love with the baby and was filling him up with so much food that he was turning into a balloon, and all the aunts did was to look kind and sad. Whenever Lucy's mother had been away before, which was almost never, and then only overnight to Scarborough or Whitby, she had always sent Lucy a postcard. But now, morning after morning, there was no post waiting on her breakfast plate. Lucy grew quiet.

One day she told Phyllis she wasn't going on the afternoon walk. Phyllis went so fast and so far and in the teeth of the wind to give the baby good strong air which Lucy hated. She hated all walks with the baby because people would stop and look at him and he was very ugly. (He grew beautiful later.)

"*Can't* I stay?"

"An' what'll you do?"

"I'll just play. I'll play actresses."

"Well, doant set place afire. And lock't doors." And she was off, full steam ahead.

Lucy locked the front door. Then she went to the kitchen and locked the back door. She got up in a chair and looked into the kitchen mirror. She made a proud and cruel face. "I am the Princess of Cleves," she said. She got down from the chair and leaning over the small fire she blacked her fingers with the soot at the fire back and drew herself a great curling moustache. "I am a pirate," she informed the cat. There was a ring at the front door bell. Lucy climbed back on the chair and drew frown lines and anger lines on her forehead and cheeks. "I'm a terrible

18

pirate," she said.

The bell pealed louder and she went and lay down on the drawing-room floor and rolled herself tightly up in the sheepskin rug so that her head stuck out one end and her sandals the other. She closed her eyes. "The Princess of Cleves is dead," she said. There was a loud rap at the window and a voice called: "LUCY—let me in this minute."

Slowly Lucy unwound herself, unbolted the door and saw that a very small, plump lady with a felt hat and a short proud nose was standing in the wallflowers. Her hair was grey, her clothes were thick and tweedy and she was carrying an enormous brown paper bag. Nothing in the world could have looked less like the rose-petal girl in the photograph: yet Lucy knew at once, that moment, that here was Auntie Kitty.

"What in the world are you?" Auntie Kitty asked.

"I-I'm Lucy."

"Are you alone?"

"Jake and Phyllis have gone for a walk. Father's at school and . . ."

"Yes?"

"Mother's . . ."

"Yes?"

"Mother's at the Fever House."

"At the WHAT?"

"Phyllis says it's the Fever House."

"It sounds dreadful!"

"It is."

"Rubbish. Come with me."

Auntie Kitty stepped carefully out of the wall-flowers and took Lucy's hand and they walked quietly through the garden and down the road to the bus-stop. Both Lucy's socks had gone to sleep in her sandals and she was wearing shorts with a tear in. She had only a thin blouse on and it was rather cold. The soot tickled.

"D'you think I ought to take my moustache off?" she asked.

"No," said Auntie Kitty. She sat firmly down in the bus with the paper bag on her knee and in no time at all the bus reached the end of the dismal wooded road and they walked up the hill to the black door that said DO NOT OPEN THIS DOOR. "What is the good of a door," said Auntie Kitty, "if you can't open it," and they marched off round a corner of the laurel hedge, down a little path and came to a wicket leading to a kitchen garden.

"I am going to tell you three things," said Auntie Kitty scanning the landscape, hand on the latch,

"Number One: This is a hospital where people go to be alone and not spread germs.

"Number Two: Children are not allowed to talk to the ill people even through the window. I think this is stupid, but it is a rule.

"Number Three: The ill people are not allowed to write letters because of germs on the paper. That is why your mother will not have written to you."

Lucy felt suddenly, wonderfully happy. "Will she get well?" she asked quite sensibly. "Come and see," said Auntie Kitty.

They went through the wicket and passed along the rows of peas. "*Good* afternoon," said Auntie Kitty to a puzzled-looking gardener, "*good* afternoon," to two very thin pale people in basket chairs and shawls, who looked quite frightened. They skirted a lavender hedge – and there was the Fever House. It was low and pretty and white with yellow roses growing all over it. Auntie Kitty paused to think, then they strode on, round a corner to a big, glassed-in verandah.

And there in a bed, looking pink and round and terribly bored sat Lucy's mother, gazing out at the garden.

Her mouth and her eyes flew wide open and her arms began to wave in all directions. She leaned over sideways, burrowed in a bag and, bouncing about on the bed, wrote on a piece of paper and held it up. It said 'Home on Monday.' She blew kisses, pulled faces and turned bright red.

Lucy began to cry. "BOO," she wailed, "BOO HOO," and her tears ran all over her moustache. "Be quiet at once," said Auntie Kitty. "Hush, you silly girl." "BOO," roared Lucy. Auntie Kitty hustled her away. "Stupid child," she snapped, almost running round a corner, over a cinder path and round the laurels to the drive and to the back of the high black door.

"BOO HOO HOO," bellowed Lucy.

21

The front door of the fever hospital opened and a huge heavy creature burst out, all navy blue with spiky white wings on its head. It had a terrible face. "*Good* afternoon," said Auntie Kitty as they slid out and were off down the hill. They could still see a little point of white standing in the road when they reached the bottom.

"Self control this instant," said Auntie Kitty, collapsing on the bus-stop bench. "Dry your face. Enough of this happiness. Then you can open the present I've brought you." It was the paper bag. After a bit of sniffing and rubbing with the back of her sleeve, Lucy opened it. Inside there seemed to be dozens and dozens of coloured cloth triangles tied together with tape.

"It's bunting. Bunting, as I would have told you at first if you hadn't gone on about Fever Houses, is flags. Flags for celebrations. You and Phyllis and that fat baby have got to decorate the whole house with this by Monday. I'll be far away by then."

Suddenly she took a handful of bunting and threw it up in the air. "Hurrah," she cried, "hurrah," and kicked up her heels. When the bus arrived the people inside were surprised to see a very dirty-faced girl and a small tweedy old lady roaring with laughter and draped in flags.

3

The Ship in the Grass

One night there was a great storm. The wind came flying over the sea. It came from the North Pole in the darkness and screamed and howled across the waves, on and on. It sent great breakers over the sands and spun the sandhills about. It flew over the church and the churchyard and the meadow and over the roof of Lucy's house where she lay in bed listening and watching the flying clouds which kept blotting out the moon. "Crack," went the slates into the yard. "Groan and crack," went branches of the sycamore trees as they lurched down. Her mother came into the room clutching her dressing-gown round her with both hands.

"Are you all right, Lucy?"

"Mmm."

"My goodness, isn't it dreadful?"

Lucy watched the sky for a long time until at last the wind began to die. Then as it started to get light the clouds moved more slowly and she went to sleep.

But when she woke the wind was up again, battering and clattering, the sun was shining hard and the sky was bright, light blue. Everything sparkled. The postman was coming up through the garden and he called to the angry maid, Phyllis, who was polishing the brass door knob:

"There's a big ship ashore."

Lucy's inside stirred.

After a minute she heard the racehorses. They passed
the house every morning for their gallop along the sands.
They first passed very early, in a string, gentle and quiet,
with the jockeys sleepy in jerseys humped upon their
backs. Then later they came back, snorting and dancing
and shaking their necks and the jockeys wide awake and
calling to each other. Lucy had been asleep for their
journey out this morning.

"There's a great ship ashore," one of them called to
Phyllis.

"Aye, I's 'eard."

A great ship, thought Lucy, but she was too sleepy
and put her head further down in the blankets.

But when she woke properly she rushed downstairs at
once and into the kitchen. "Lucy, there's a big . . ."
began her father. "Yes I know. Can we go now?"

"Now? Now? Never in the world. Have your
breakfast."

"Mother!" She rushed into the back yard. "Mother,
there's a huge . . ."

"Yes dear," said her mother, lifting her face into the
cold wind and looking at the galloping golden clouds.
"What a splendid day for drying blankets."

"Can we go now?"

"Of course not. Much too soon."

Lucy hopped and fussed and fretted and begged.

"It might be gone."

"Never. Do get out of the way, dear."

"It mightn't be true."

"I'm sure it's true. It will wait an hour. Do take that peg off your nose. It will leave a mark."

"Well, can I go alone? Over the sandhills? I'll take care. PLEASE."

"No Lucy, most certainly not. You must wait until you've had your breakfast, and then we'll go together."

So it was nearly the middle of the morning when Lucy and her mother at last set off to see the ship across the sandhills – but they saw it long before they thought they would. You could see it from the churchyard itself – great masts and a funnel sticking up just behind the stile. Yet really it was far across the sands on the sea's edge.

"OH!" they both cried, "it's *enormous*."

They walked across the shining wet sand. Other people were coming from all directions like insects gathering for a feast. They met in little clusters round the great red ship and looked up and up to the deck far away.

"They was Chinamen," said an old fisherman. "Terrible sailors, Chinamen. They've all bin took away. They went to Middlesbrough on a train early on."

Lucy walked all round the ship. It was standing up quite straight like a decoration on a Christmas cake. From a distance it looked as if it was standing on top of the sand, but nearby you saw that it was in a deep trough full of sea water. It had thrust itself into the sand on a great wave and was left all by itself in a long, ship-shaped pond. There were ugly, rusty trickly marks down the sides and crusty shells on the bottom half of it – the part that was not meant to be seen. Suddenly, high above, a black face looked down at Lucy under a mop of shining hair. Fierce eyes flashed and a bucket of rubbish was thrown overboard to land in the pond.

"Disgusting!" everybody said.

"Chinamen," said the fisherman.

"He doesn't look like a Chinaman," said Lucy. "He's black."

"Believe me," said the fisherman, "he'll be a Chinaman and the sooner he's away the better."

"But how will it ever *go*?" fussed Lucy at dinner-time. "It'll never move again. It'll be there for ever. Will we be able to climb up? Will somebody buy it to live in? It's as long as a street. Father, how did it come? How does it stand so straight?"

"Oh, do go slower, dear," said her mother. "And a ship is called 'she'."

"The reasons are called 'Physics'," said her father in the voice of a schoolmaster.

"Shall we go again? Shall we go after dinner? Can you come, too, Father? Can Jake miss his rest? Can . . .?"

"Lucy, take the plates. Go upstairs, take off your shoes and lie down on your bed for half an hour. You sound quite wild."

"Oh I couldn't. I couldn't sleep. I couldn't."

"Then read a book."

"No, I . . ."

"Or go to the aunts."

"Oh," said Lucy. "Oh yes. I'd like to go to the aunts. Can I go now? Please may I?"

"YES YOU MAY," said her parents and gave great sighs as she vanished from the house.

The aunts lived very near in a lovely house with big windows, looking over the cricket field and the Cleveland Hills. One of the windows in the top was oval and had glass petals like an oval daisy. When you went into this house you became calm. It was quiet and smelled sweetly of apples and bread baking. The aunts were always at home in the afternoon, sitting in the drawing-room in their hats.

"Now go out again," said Aunt Fanny, "and come back properly. You're like the north wind." Aunt Fanny had a mouth like a purse done up with a drawstring, and very little chin. She was thin and her big eyes were like a monkey's – beautifully sad; though she could be full of larks.

"Well now, dear!" said Auntie Bea. "How lovely." She was plump and good and happy.

"Did you know," said Lucy puffing and flopping, "there's a HUGE ship on the sands. Just standing there. Nearly on the golf links. Just standing. Huge!"

"Is there, dear?"

"Huge. High as a church. There's a Chinaman on it with a bucket with black hair and crowds and crowds. There's never been such a thing. The sea behind it is all shallow and miles away. The reason is Physics. It must have taken a leap like a circus. It's marvellous. Like a miracle."

"Now Lucy dear . . ."

"LUCY!"

Lucy stopped.

"Lucy, I simply can't do with this fussing. Sit still and I'll read you 'The Queen of the May'!" Aunt Fanny picked up a velvety green book with gold writing on it and began to turn the flimsy pages, with her knobbly hands.

"I hate 'The Queen of the May'."

There was a silence. "I see," said Aunt Fanny who read it to her often.

"Oh, I'm sorry," said Lucy. "I'm sorry. It's just I do so want to tell you about this ship."

"Oh Lucy." Aunt Fanny looked at Auntie Bea and Auntie Bea looked at Aunt Fanny. "What does it remind you of?" And they both began to laugh.

"What's the matter?" asked Lucy.

"Nothing," said Auntie Bea. "Just that it's all happened before – so many times. Auntie Fan and I have lived here seventy years, you know. You forget how old the sea is and how old ships are. And the sands are as old as the world nearly."

"Yes, but you haven't *seen* it. It's huge and red, all barnacles and rust marks and a great fat funnel like a gas works . . ."

"Well, there have been some beautiful ships," said Aunt Fanny looking out of the window at the hills beyond the cricket field, and the wild sky. "Beautiful. There was the ship in the grass."

"What's the ship in the grass?"

"Sit down," said Aunt Fanny suddenly, "in that little chair. Don't move until I say and while you are waiting to be calm I will tell you about the ship in the grass. Do you remember, Bea?"

"Well of course I do."

"Now then –

"Once upon a time, a very long time ago and don't unravel the cushion, before I was born – long before – there was a tremendous storm. Last night we had a storm but it was nothing like this one. The roof flew off the church and fell in among the graves. The old village school beside the golf links there nearly disappeared. The sandhills all changed their shapes and the high was made low and the low was raised up like the Psalms. All the little fishermen's cottages in Coatham High Street filled up with sand like rabbit holes and they had to dig themselves out. And when they had dug themselves out, there was a little sailing ship perched high up on top of the sandhills, all by itself, like Noah's Ark on Ararat.

"It was a lovely little ship. Its sails were torn to ribbons, but there it stood like a seagull, all fresh and wet and beautiful. As far as you could see there was nobody on board. Not a sign of life. There were very few people here in those days – it was a lonely place – and such as there were I suppose came and had a look, and because it

31

was perched up so high as if a breath of wind would send it toppling, they didn't look too closely. They just went on with their lives. It stayed on top of its little hill week after week and month after month and grass grew all around it out of the sand – you know that silvery sharp grass that cuts you if you get hold of it too tight. Everyone called it 'the ship in the grass' and after a while it became just like the palms of their hands and they stopped seeing it.

"Well, one day your Great-Aunt Sarah – no, she'd be your great-great-aunt, because we are your great-aunts. Or was she our great-aunt? – never mind. Aunt Sarah was running along the beach with Uncle Alfred, bowling a hoop. She was wearing a long skirt like a bell and long frilly pantaloons and he was in a sailor suit. The sand was coming along with them like smoke in long curly lines and the hoops simply flew and they could hardly keep up. They found they were near the ship in the grass and they noticed all of a sudden that the sand had piled up on one side, right up so that you might be able to get on board. Up went Alfred. He clutched on to a porthole first, then he cartwheeled over and leaned down for your Aunt Sarah and over she went in the bell skirt and thumped down on the deck. And the little ship never trembled.

"They ran about and looked down the hatchways and into the cabin. Aunt Sarah said there were lots of little brass pots and pans still hanging on the hooks, all turned bright green with the salt water. Alfred took the tiller and called 'Ship Ahoy!' and Aunt Sarah said, 'Let's play

Nelson.' Alfred put his left arm in his sailor suit and shut an eye and pretended to look through a telescope. 'Bang!' shouted Aunt Sarah and down fell Lord Nelson. 'Oh!' he cried, 'I am dead. Kiss me Hardy. England expects this day that every man shall do his duty.' 'Oh, oh,' wailed Aunt Sarah, turning into Nelson's friend. 'Oh – Nelson is dead. The greatest Englishman. Lost for ever.'

"'A cock sparrow.'

"'What did you say, Alfred?'

"'Nothing. You did.'

"'No – somebody said, "A cock sparrow".'

"They were very frightened. 'It's a ghost,' said Aunt Sarah, and they listened.

"'Nelson were a cock sparrow,' said the voice again from quite nearby. Sitting in the prow they suddenly noticed an old man sucking a short white pipe and looking past them at the sea.

"'Nelson,' he said, 'were a cock sparrow and I should know for I were there. Strutting about, the deck over, medals a-glittering, cockade a-flying. There's a Frenchie up a rigging sees a glitter far off and he aims his gun and down goes Nelson – but you see he *would go dressing up*. Oh, there was weeping – and below decks, too. But he were a cock sparrow.'

"Aunt Sarah and Uncle Alfred went up to the old man then and they could see he was very old indeed. He was as dry and thin as the ship's timbers. His eyes were bright blue with crimson lines round them and his hair was puffy and white and his face, she said, was as brown as tea and as threaded with lines as an old leaf. He said no more to them and after a while they went home. Aunt Sarah said they didn't tell anyone for ever so long because they weren't sure if they'd dreamed it all."

"Had they?" asked Lucy.

"No. There was an old man who used to break stones in Redcar Lane and I believe he *had* been on the *Victory*. He'd been pressed aboard when he was young and how he'd wandered this way goodness knows. Yes – your Great-Great-Aunt Sarah really did meet someone on our sands who had seen the death of Lord Nelson himself."

"And what happened to the ship in the grass?" said Lucy who wasn't very good at History.

"My dear," said Auntie Bea, "if you could just unroll yourself from the hearth rug. I feel sure it is dusty . . ."

"The ship in the grass," said Aunt Fanny leaning forward and tweaking her out. "The ship in the grass got covered with sand I expect."

Lucy erupted from the hearth rug completely and sat like a rod.

"Do you mean it's still there?"

"I expect so, dear. It was when we were young, wasn't it, Bea?"

"Oh yes, I think so. But perhaps we just remember Aunt Sarah telling us. I *think* we saw it. Dear me, it does seem so long . . ."

"D'you mean that if I went looking I might find it? And

the portholes? And the little pots on hooks? And the cupboards still all full of things?"

"You might."

"And treasures? I might find treasures? Gold and swords and jewels and things and pieces-of-eight?"

"I'm not sure about pieces-of-eight, but you never know."

"Oh my goodness!"

But Lucy never did. She only found seagulls' feathers and bed springs and driftwood and sea-coal and nasty bits of buried newspaper and a pram with three wheels and a rusty spiky bicycle and once an old thin brass button.

And the big, red ship disappeared, too. When Lucy came back from her summer holidays at Thornby End it was gone. The sands were smooth and empty. The racehorses danced like insects on the edge of the sea and one or two sea-coal gatherers went slowly about near the breakwater; and the only marks in the sandhills were made by her own feet.

4

Mr Crossley's Wig

Aunt Fanny and Auntie Bea had decided, some years before Lucy was born, that it is very difficult to live without any money. They had some very fine chairs, some beautiful china teacups, and a family tree in a black box, but in the bank they found, all of a sudden, that they had no money at all. Not a sixpence. Not a threepenny piece.

So they decided to take in paying summer visitors, and after saying so to one or two people, paying summer visitors began to pour in from every side because they loved Lucy's great aunts and knew that if they didn't pay the rent the aunts would be far too polite to ask them to leave.

The house was soon full, and Aunt Fanny and Auntie Bea began to slave and slave, ordering and cooking and making lists and managing, and soon they took in an extra maid who began to slave too, and everyone was happy and Aunt Fanny said, "Bea, if this goes on we shall all have new dresses for Christmas."

Lucy used to stand behind the curtains in the Aunts' drawing-room – between the inner and the outer curtains – and watch the visitors as they appeared each summer up the garden path; and as the same visitors seemed to come back and back she used to look out for old faces – like the faces of Mrs. Hinton and Mrs. Hinton's nurse.

And they, as her father said, had not got faces but faces-and-a-half.

The nurse always appeared first with a flinging open of the gate, a big brown woman with a satisfied look that said: 'Look at me! I'm doing some good in this world. See how I manage this troublesome old lady!' Then a great hustling and creaking and the taxi man and his assistant set down a huge wicker chair on wheels with a great roll of rugs in it and at the top of the roll, nidding and nodding and smiling to herself under a huge black straw hat, sat Mrs. Hinton. All you could see of her face was a big polished old chin with little holes in it and an overhanging nose with a long, long water drop on the end. As she came bowling up the path she looked a little to the left and a little to the right and said, "How nice the flowers look." Then she settled down for three months in a bed-sitting room the aunts had made on the ground floor and did enormous jigsaws from morning till night and the nurse sat beside her, knitting. Knitting that is, and pinging away at the bell by the fireplace for every single thing you could think of.

One day a very well-dressed old gentleman appeared at the front door when Lucy was hanging aimlessly about the drawing-room curtains. He had gold eye-glasses the shape of the orange and lemon slices you eat after Christmas dinner, a pale suit, spats and a pink carnation; and he asked for a private talk with Miss Fanny and Miss

Bea. Lucy, who was staying the day as she always did on Saturdays, was shooed off upstairs. From her favourite top window – the one shaped like an oval glass daisy – she watched him half an hour later go away down the path again, shooting out his walking-stick ahead of him and swaying his shoulders as if he were very pleased. There was something or other about him that reminded Lucy of the nurse.

He had called, it seemed, to make arrangements for a relative of his, a Mr. Crossley, who was shortly coming to work in the family firm a few miles away in Middlesbrough. "We are Shipping," he said, "ahem, Shipping."

"I see," said Aunt Fanny. "What kind of Shipping do you, er . . .?"

"Oh, quite general. General Shipping."

"That must be a most interesting profession," said Aunt Fanny.

"My relative – my nephew – has lived a very quiet life. Yes – very quiet. We think that the time has come for him however to, er, break free. To stand as one might say upon his own feet. In the care, of course, of good Christian folk, ladies such as yourselves."

"Why of course," said Miss Fanny.

"Is he very young?" asked Auntie Bea. "I should love to cook for somebody young again. Does he play cricket? Boys do get so splendidly hungry after cricket. Our cricket field you know is just across the way."

"No, no. Not what you would call young," said the

41

elderly gentleman. "Well, fiftyish. And *very* quiet. You do understand, really *very* quiet indeed. Quite happy to be alone in his room. And a very *small* appetite, I am afraid."

"How long will he be wanting to stay?" asked Aunt Fanny rather blankly.

"Oh forever," said the old gentleman. "And I would suggest thirty shillings a week."

"Well, what could I say?" Aunt Fanny asked the ceiling later. "Thirty shillings a week and no appetite! It is a fortune. Nobody has ever paid more than fifteen and Mrs. Hinton only pays nine and sixpence because of knowing Dolly Thwaites's cousin in Harrogate. And *forever*!"

"There's something a bit funny about it if you ask me," said another aunt who had dropped in on her way from a Church Council Meeting – Auntie Gladys who saw through most things. "I expect he dribbles."

"Poor Mrs. Hinton dribbles," said Aunt Fanny.

"We shall all dribble one day," said gentle Auntie Bea.

But Mr. Crossley did not dribble. He was tall, upright and thin, rather youngish-looking for his age, with a solid brown moustache very thick and neat. He was as beautifully dressed as his uncle and wore cream gloves fastened with little amber-coloured press studs. He carried a well-polished little case, and wore a large grey hat with a dent down the middle and a broad, black ribbon round it. He removed this carefully, bowed to the aunts, and was shown to his room.

Every morning he had a very small breakfast taken up to him on a tray and precisely at a quarter to nine he set off down the main stairs with his little case, his hat already upon his head, to catch his train. He returned about six, went straight upstairs, washed, changed into a linen jacket and awaited his supper tray. Then there was absolute silence until Doris, the younger maid, took up his hot-water can at bedtime. She said he was always sitting with a book he did not seem to be enjoying very much or just standing, looking out of the window and jingling the money in his pockets.

"Can I take his tray? May I? May I?" Lucy begged, and Doris let her once. She had to put it on the floor before she knocked and pick it up again after she had heard him say, "Ahem," which she thought probably meant "Come in." The door swung open with a bit of a rush and she nearly got lost in the folds of the green chenille curtain that hung behind it; but at last she burst through to see him sitting deep in his armchair, his knees up in points and his queer, pale eyes looking at her hard.

"He's a bit creepy."

"I'll say he's creepy!"

"That'll do, Doris," said Ada Binns. She had been with the aunts for twenty years and Doris scarcely one.

"Why'll it do?" (Doris was rude.) "What's wrong with saying he's creepy? I think he's a hescaped mur-

43

derer his family's trying to hide. Never says nothing. Never does nothing."

"He does then, Doris Duckering. He goes to his work every day with that beautiful attatchy case and never misses. He's a real gentleman whatever else he isn't."

"I never said he wasn't. All I sez is he's a bit, well, so-so. And that attatchy case is empty if you want to know, 'cos I looked in it once when he'd gone to the bathroom."

"Doris Duckering, you can just keep quiet – and take that cigarette out of your mouth when you're on duty of an afternoon."

But Lucy saw that Ada was uneasy.

"And I'll tell you somethink else," said Doris, flouncing off with an enormous scuttle of coal for the nurse, and pushing a bent cigarette into her apron pocket, "he wears a wig."

"What's 'so-so'?" Lucy asked her parents at Sunday dinner.

"Not very well," said her mother.

"Or not very good," said her father.

"Can it mean, well, mad?"

"Yes, I suppose it could. Yes, people do say 'A bit so-so', don't they?"

"Could you say that Mr. Crossley was a bit so-so?"

"Have another Yorkshire." Her mother began hastily waving a dish about.

"He's not so-so," said her father. "He's barmy!"

"William!"

"Plain barmy. And I'll tell you something else about him. He wears a wig."

Lucy pondered.

"I've heard some *very* funny stories about that Mr. Crossley," was the next thing she overheard. Auntie Gladys had dropped in on her way back from the Church Working Party. She settled down, dropped the corners of her mouth and shifted about in her chair once or twice from the waist downwards. "Off you go, Lucy." Her mother gave her a look. Lucy lingered.

"They say he just sits in that family office in Middlesbrough all day reading the paper. They've given him a desk for the look of the thing. He's not right, you know."

"Oh come, Gladys!"

"Oh I'm not saying he's bad enough to be put away, of course, but he's definitely odd. He's definitely so-so. And do you know, Kathleen, he wears a wig!"

"Whoever's the new lodger?" asked Mrs. Hinton's nurse, come the Spring. "Can't say I care for him much." Lucy was hanging over the jigsaw.

"He is of very good family," said Aunt Fanny, bridling.

"And the very *easiest* of guests," said Auntie Bea.

"Well, he wears a wig," squawked Mrs. Hinton suddenly. (It was as if the earth had spoken.) "Give me that

45

bit of sky, girl. He wears a wig! He wears a wig!" She cackled and screamed. "Oh-ho! He wears a wig!"

"And whatever's the matter," said Lucy to her best and most particular friend, Mary Fell, "with wearing a wig?" They were talking in one of the old greenhouses of the empty house across the road from Lucy's, a house called Dennis. It was a place of gloom and great over-grown creeping plants like cushions of cress that had swelled and spread all over the peeling benches and rusty pipes, and taken root in the very walls along with sweet brown wallflowers and bruisable foxgloves – a steamy, peaceful place very good for conversations. "I'd love to wear a wig. I mean, look at Charles the First. Everyone thinks he was marvellous, but I bet nobody knows what he *looked* like without a wig. His wig was part of his looking marvellous. And yet there's poor old Mr. Crossley . . ."

"Charles the First had a different face," said Mary.

"It wasn't all that different. His eyes were darker, I suppose, but they've both got that funny, sad look. D'you think his moustache is a wig, too?"

"No, I think that's growing. I was having a good look in church the other day. I couldn't get a steady look because he sits at the back, but I kept turning round and sort of concentrating now and then. I don't know what it is they mean about his hair anyway. You can hardly see it really. It must have been an awfully cheap one if it's a

46

wig. You'd think he'd have got a good big one while he was about it. They all seem sure though."

"You'd think it was something really awful the way they go on. I mean they don't make all that carry-on about false teeth."

"It seems to sort of ... fascinate them, somehow."

They thought about it.

"Mind you," said Mary Fell, "I'm glad my father hasn't got one."

"Would you like to marry someone with one?"

They shuddered and shook.

"We're as bad as they are," said Mary. "You see, we wouldn't."

"Would we if it was King Charles the First?"

"Not even then. Not even to be queen. Not even to be Princess of Cleves."

"The Princess of Cleves," said Lucy, looking down her nose, "has wigs of her own. One for weekdays, two for Sundays." She picked up an eiderdown of cress and arranged it on her head. "Made of emeralds," she said, "bits of topaz," she picked a wallflower and some foxgloves, "rubies, pearls and sad, white opals." She stuck them here and there and put a foxglove over each finger tip and clawed the air.

"You're mad," said Mary Fell.

"I'm so-so," said Lucy.

The year went rolling on.

One night in summer, Lucy and Mary were on a visit to the aunts for a treat, staying the night up in the attic with the pretty window. The house had two attics with a very steep, narrow staircase in between, and in the back attic slept Ada and Doris. "So you won't be lonely," said Auntie Bea, "and after all Aunt Fanny and I are not so very, very far away. Goodness! What a hot night!"

After she had gone, shutting the door carefully behind her to keep out the maids' chatter, Lucy and Mary got out of their covers and lay on the top of their beds. They talked on and on, watching the light go away from the oval daisy, wondering about various things like what made Mrs. Hinton like jigsaw puzzles and what made Ada so cross all the time with Doris and why it would have seemed odd if the aunts had ever had husbands. After a while they got back to Mr. Crossley. "Doris says he never sleeps. Something must be fussing him an awful lot. I wonder what it is?" But Mary was asleep at last and didn't answer and soon Lucy was asleep, too, listening as she dropped off to Doris's high voice going on and on in a quarrelsome sort of way across the landing.

She woke up and smelled smoke.

She sat up and sniffed and then found herself coughing. She jumped out of bed and opened the door and a great cloud of smoke lay thick upon the stairs. She slammed it to. "Oh help! Goodness! Mary – quick!"

Together they tried to open the only pane of glass in the window that had a little hinge. "Help! Fire!" they cried, but nobody heard except the birds asleep upon the cricket pavilion and the cricket field trees far below.

A million pins pricked Lucy all over from her scalp to her soles and she felt herself blushing with fear. "Oh what shall we do?" they both said, and looked at each other. Mary's solemn clever face looked swimmy in the darkness. "I don't know," she said.

Below, in their bedrooms towards the back of the house, the aunts slept peacefully with their windows wide open for health, Aunt Fanny on a hard straw palliasse, Auntie Bea on feathers and three pillows. On the floor below Mrs. Hinton slept as deeply, dreaming of Harrogate and bread-and-milk and wisps of the scenes of great balls she had attended when she was a girl. In the dark little room beside the pantry the nurse slept soundly, too, and made a great deal of noise doing it. Otherwise the house was still, with only now and then a petal falling from the flower vases, silently onto the floor. And upstairs the smoke grew thicker and there was a sudden dreadful crackling.

"Oh Mary," said Lucy, with tears coming like a baby's, "I don't know what to do."

But somebody did. From the best bedroom on the landing below them suddenly sprang – Mr. Crossley. In two steps he was over it and had opened the door to the attic staircase. One look and he shut it, vanished into his bedroom and reappeared with his face in a wet cloth and carrying a blanket and a water jug.

49

"Bea!" came a shriek from below, "Oh Bea! There's a fire!" and the aunts were there upon the main staircase in their nightdresses, their hands pressed tight against their faces. "Oh Fanny, Fanny, the children!"

Mr. Crossley leapt at the staircase again like a horse into battle and disappeared. There was a clump, a bump, a kick, a crash, and a long splashing noise and various moans: then down he rushed again carrying a bundle wrapped in a blanket. He dashed past them to the hall. "Don't be afraid," he cried, "I'm going to drown it in the water butt." And away he went, knees-bent like a grass-hopper.

"What on earth!" said Auntie Bea. "D'you know Fanny I think he really must be mad."

"Whatever was in the blanket?" said Aunt Fanny. "Oh dear, I hope it wasn't Lucy!"

It wasn't, however, for Lucy arrived at that moment out of the smoke which was already thinning, followed by Mary Fell followed by Ada Binns followed by Doris Duckering who was howling into a handkerchief. "It was that Doris's cigarettes," said Ada in a loud voice. "I'll say it now and I'll say it on the Judgement Day. I've tellt her and I've tellt her. There now. That's what it was." All four of them were shaking. "She throws them in the waste-paper basket. Every night she does it."

"I thought it was out, I did honest," wept Doris.

"All is well." Mr. Crossley reappeared from the bowels

of the house. His tie was under his ear and his hands were black but he was otherwise as neat as ever. Yet there seemed to be something different about him.

"Mr. Crossley," Miss Fanny went up to him and took both his dirty hands in her own little knobbly ones. "Mr. Crossley, my dear, dear Mr. Crossley! You have saved our lives. You are the best and bravest of men. And oh, my dear Mr. Crossley . . . (Doris at this point suddenly gave a long, slow howl and pointed to Mr. Crossley as he bent slightly over Miss Fanny's hand) . . . I am afraid that the fire has quite burned off your hair."

Mr. Crossley stiffened. Then he loosed his hands and timidly felt his head. His face seemed to have turned to wood. "It will never grow again," said Miss Fanny. "The shock . . . in these cases I believe that it never does." Mr. Crossley did not move. "Oh Mr. Crossley," said Auntie Bea, "I do believe it suits you better."

And a great and magnificent smile broke over Mr. Crossley's face and he bowed to everyone in a very stately way and went off to his room.

They found it of course the next morning after he had left for work. "Miss Fanny, Miss Bea!" screamed Doris (she had been told to go the night before but the aunts had relented after breakfast on condition that she gave up smoking). "There's a nasty, queer, brown thing a-hangin' on the line." And there it was, caught in a stray clothes-peg as Mr. Crossley had rushed with the burning

51

waste-paper basket under the washing-line in the darkness. It looked a sad, silly little bit of hair, with an inside
like a thrush's nest and little juicy bits to hold it on.

"I can't bear it! I cannot endure!" Aunt Fanny suddenly cried and went flying off to collapse somewhere
upon a sofa, but kind Auntie Bea said, "Fanny, for
shame! It is not funny in the very least. Lucy, fetch me the
sugar tongs and Mary Fell dear, fetch me the little brown
trowel from the shed." And they buried it in the garden
and grew crocuses over it.

"Nice flowers," said Mrs. Hinton next Spring-time,
nid-nodding up the path.

"We planted them in memory of dear Mr. Crossley, the
morning after the fire, don't you remember?"

"In memory? Has he gone then?" asked the nurse
hopefully.

"Gone? Good gracious no. But he goes about a great
deal now you know – to the cricket, the Operatics, and
only this morning Cousin Gladys was saying when she
dropped in on her way to the Quiet Day with the Vicar,
that he is to be made a Sidesman. He will be carrying the
plate by Lady Day. Oh dear me, we hardly see him now."

"I suppose he's still a bit so-so?"

"So-so?" Aunt Fanny pursed up her mouth.

"Well, not quite like other people?"

"Oh, not in the very least like other people. I see what
you mean, Nurse. (Come along now, up we go. Mind the

umbrella-stand. Mrs. Hinton, let me help with your hat pins.) Not in the least like other people I am glad to say. He is kinder, braver and very much more interesting. We hope that he will stay with us forever. Until the end of his life."

And of course he did.

5

The Tinker at the Door

A little cart came down the lonning of Thornby End and there was a knock at the kitchen door. "Missis," shouted Milly (Grandmother's girl), "it's the Tinkers," and the Missis came running.

She loved the Tinkers because they told fortunes. She believed every word they said and so did Milly. This tinker was a small brown one with curly hair, and he leaned against the doorpost of the farm with his foot on the step that had a long dip in the middle from many, many years of clogs and boots.

The Missis chose a small pot from the cart – the Tinkers are sometimes called Potters in this part of Cumberland – and a dear little basket chair with prickly black nails sticking out all over it so that when you got up it got up with you, and over the years collected so many coloured scraps of wool from people's cardigans that it began to look like a hedge in Spring.

The Tinker was very pleased indeed to sell all this and told them they were going to have very good luck. He gave Milly a length of blue ribbon with cream roses sewn on it and he gave the Missis a large, square envelope with a lot of black writing on it. It made a sandy noise when she shook it.

"Whativver is this?" she asked.

"It's a shampoo."

"Whativver is that?"

"It's for washing the hair."

"Instead of soap?"

"Why aye. All ladies use shampoo."

"It sounds Chinese," said the Missis and she stood on the kitchen fender and propped the envelope on the high mantelpiece among the tea tins with the faded pictures of the last king and queen on them. And there it stayed for weeks and weeks and weeks.

It stayed there until the morning of the day when Lucy and her parents and her little brother Jake were arriving for the school holidays. Lucy and Jake were very fortunate children because their grandparents lived on a beautiful farm in Cumberland among the mountains. Thornby End was not all humped down in a hollow in the mountains in the mist and rain – it stood in wide rolling countryside and out of the front windows you could see the whole of a great, purple mountain called Skidder which had a patch of snow near the top even at haytime. Out of the back windows in winter and from the bottom of the orchard in summer you could see another great, floating shadowy mountain called Criffel, and this was in Scotland. Clean clouds flew across the sky, clean white curtains blew at the windows. The beds were fourposters and there were roses painted on all the china.

Since Lucy's father had such long holidays they spent a good deal of time at Thornby End and the days they set out there were wonderful. They travelled in five different steam trains, right over the back of England from the east to the west, slowly up and up the Pennine fells ("I *think* I can, I *think* I can") and steadily and clankily down the other side ("I *knew* I could, I *knew* I could") beside the stony River Eden. It was usually almost evening when they arrived. The last train stopped a great many times at stations that seemed to spend most of their time fast asleep and when at last they reached their own station, the train would sigh and fall absolutely silent as if it could never move again. The station master would come along to their carriage with a little flight of steps to set them down, for the platform was short, and after they had shaken hands twice all round and they had watched the train at last steam away, they walked across the lines, hauled each other up the other side and Grandfather would be waiting for them in the farm cart pulled either by the brown horse or the grey one.

They rolled away down the lane, Father and Grandfather talking about the fields they were passing and the state of the corn; down to a farm called Green Rigg, turned right along the road to Waverton, and there was the big white gate. Thornby End was two fields off, on the same level as the gate, but to reach it you had to go sharp down and sharp up the lonning that led to it. There was a pond on the left of the lonning at the bottom, and on the right a spinney, and at the top of the lonning, right in the middle, the Missis, Lucy and Jake's grandmother, always stood waiting for them.

She had stood waiting for them there ever since Lucy could remember. She was a tiny old lady, hardly bigger than Lucy, but she was very perfect, with everything just right about her, so that other bigger people felt huge and awkward. She had very bright brown eyes, very black arched eyebrows which she cut with the scissors, and wonderful, white silky hair which she wore piled high on her beautiful, small head. She had a little straight nose like a duchess. When she saw the cart come into sight she would begin to raise her arms in the air and drop them down again and call out strange words. "Lorgan-days," she would cry, and "Well ivvever!" Lucy would climb down to open the gate and then go tearing down the lonning and up the lonning to be the first to reach her.

Now on this particular July day, Lucy, Jake and their parents reached Leegate station and got into the cart with their grandfather who was sucking his teeth a bit, looking straight ahead and not saying much. He was called "a tempestuous, difficult man" and sometimes he had his own thoughts. Down the lane they went, past Green Rigg, along the Waverton road to the white lonning gate – and the Missis was not there.

She was not there. The lonning was empty.

"Wherever's Mamma?" asked Lucy's father.

"She's aloft."

"Aloft?"

"Aye – she's above."

He said no more. Lucy thought, Can she be dead? Is

that what he means? But it didn't seem likely because her grandfather began to sing. "Oh where did you get that hat, that hat," he sang. (It was his only song.)

When they got round to the kitchen door out rushed Milly. "Come in now, come in!" she cried. "Oh it's a terrible thing." Her eyes were bright but the corners of her mouth didn't know what to do. She seemed to be both laughing and crying and she blinked a good deal. "Lan' sakes! Come in now, come in."

They trooped in to where tea was laid on the huge dining table that nearly filled the room. A rich red furry cloth with hanging bobbles on it was covered as usual with a shiny white cloth of double damask and on this were plate-cakes of apple and plum and tea cakes and cherry cakes, a ham and great big lopsided tomatoes and huge glass dishes of raspberry jam. But nobody seemed hungry. Grandfather lay back in his chair gazing past the tall geraniums on the window-ledge at the sky.

After a while Milly said, "Ye'd better come up then," and they all filed out except for Grandfather. As they closed the door on him they heard a queer noise. You'd have said it was a chuckle if he had been a chuckling man.

They trooped into her grandmother's bedroom and there she sat with her tiny feet drawn up on the rung of an upright chair. She was wearing neat little buttoned black slippers like Lucy's and a little high round collar with a frill on top, a gold brooch with three corals in it, and against the black silk of her afternoon dress hung a fine gold chain and a round little watch as thin as a biscuit. She was looking out at the mountains through the stiff lace curtains, tied back with blue tapes, sitting as straight as an empress. But her head was wrapped up in a bit of old blanket.

"Lorgan-days!" she said. "Well ivvever!" But she didn't look at them. She stared at the mountains very, very sadly.

There was a pause and then Milly said, "Come on now, Missis, it'll have to come off," and she leaned forward and tweaked off the blanket.

There was the wonderful hair – silky and shining and wound high up on her head. But it was bright green.

It was the colour of cooking-apples.

Not until much later in the day did it come out. Everybody got to work on the poor Missis. They scrubbed and they rubbed with hard squares of dark yellow soap – the kind you don't see any more these days. Then they rinsed and they rinsed with soft rainwater from the butt by the stackyard gate and at last it was almost white again. Very late that evening they all sat round the kitchen – not Jake for he was in bed, and not Milly who was out with her young man, but the others – in the lamplight and the firelight, talking and listening to the noises of mice in the stick-oven. The stars were out through the window and the Missis was full of all kinds of news. She talked and nodded, she nodded and talked. Her eyes were bright, her face was rosy and her hair hung down in a cloud.

"Whativver did she want with yon foreign things?" said Grandfather suddenly breaking into the talk. "Heathen packages. Whativver did she *do* it for?"

The Missis said she wouldn't be doing it again, and just wait till she saw that Tinker.

But she never did.

6

The Beast in the Mire

Lucy and the Missis, her grandmother, were going out to tea. It was a heavy afternoon, burning and still. The cows in the Rough Ground stood looking too exhausted to flick their tails at the flies that were almost too exhausted to bother them. Only their lower jaws went round and round and round and their eyes were full of prayers for rain.

It was the strangest September. For weeks the sun had shone on the wet green fields of Cumberland and turned them dry and brown. The purple mountains became rabbit-coloured, the threads of becks disappeared from their slopes and every morning the early mist turned into a burning, glaring day. Week after week after week it went on.

Lucy's father was helping his brother with the threshing over Bromfield way and her mother had taken Jake on the bus to the sea at Silloth, twenty miles off. Lucy hadn't wanted to go with them. As a matter of fact she hadn't wanted to do anything all day. She had a cold and her eyes were streaming and her nose, and she hung about the farm in a funny sort of mood. "Hangy," said Milly, Grandmother's girl, "Lucy's hangy, that's what." At dinner-time she pushed her food about and knocked the table leg until her grandfather roared at her.

"For shame, William. The child has cold," said her grandmother.

"Cold this weather? Cold? Land sakes!" He went to the kitchen door and looked across the glaring farm-yard where the sheep dog lay like an old hearth-rug in the shadow of the water butt. "Cold!" he said and went off to lie on top of the kist in the back kitchen with the yellow blind pulled down behind his head. "Cold!" he said, and fell asleep.

"I'll tell you what," said the Missis, "we'll away off to tea with Mabel Twentyman. Just you and me, Lucy. We'll take the bus."

Milly stopped washing dishes and turned round. "Think on," she said, "think on."

"Yes, yes, yes," said the Missis, tippetting about. "Come along now and change your frock and I'll change mine and we'll go across the Rough Ground by Sappy Moss and be up at the bus-stop by two o'clock."

"Ye never will!"

"We will for sure."

So there they were toiling up the Rough Ground in the heat of the day, Granny in her black stockings and long coat and black straw hat with the veil tied under the chin, and Lucy in a clean cotton dress with her nose running and the cows trying to keep their eyes open to watch them.

"Why did Milly say 'Think on'?" Lucy flopped down in the front seat of the bus upstairs where you bounced about on the corners and the branches thumped the roof overhead.

"Tut tut. Up straight," said the Missis, stiff as thistles. "Ladies never slump."

"But why did Milly say 'Think on'?" She began to wind the window up and down.

"Dear, dear! Ladies never go out without gloves," said the Missis, smoothing her own little black leather ones which would have about fitted one of Lucy's dolls.

"And no hat neither," she added. "Because Mabel Twentyman's a witch, that's why."

It was hotter than ever when they were set down at the lane end and the fields seemed to be rippling and melting before Lucy's eyes. You could see the house they were going to at once, half-way up the fell with its windows shining. It looked miles away. But the Missis was over the stile and away with a smile on her face under the veil, so Lucy trudged behind, and when at last they reached the white iron gates, there was the witch standing waiting for them at her front door.

It was the most surprising house for a witch, with a gravel drive and ugly modern windows such as you might see on the outskirts of Carlisle; and really the most surprising witch in charge of it. She was just like Lucy's maths mistress (which was a bad start) and she was wearing a neat blue skirt, a pale silk blouse with a long string of pearls round her neck. Her hair was curled very tightly in even waves and she wore gleaming spectacles. She had gingerish silk stockings, highly polished shoes with laces, and a sensible mouth.

"There's a cake on the table," she said.

"Lorgan-days, Mabel!" said the Missis. "A cake! Why we never said we was coming, but I just had the feeling."

"Aye, I was expecting you. The cake's on the table and there'll be tea right away."

"And this is Lucy," said the Missis.

Lucy held out her hot hand and looked at Mabel Twentyman and Mabel Twentyman looked at Lucy but did not take it. Lucy looked into Mabel Twentyman's eyes behind the spectacles and Mabel Twentyman looked back. And they did not like each other. Mabel Twentyman's round, clear, pale eyes looked into Lucy's hot face very hard and long and Lucy felt a great and hideous shiver go down her back. Yes, she is a witch, she thought. Oh I want to go home.

Without a word Mabel Twentyman turned away. "Come along, Elizabeth, and have your tea. Lucy would rather stay in the garden. She shall have her tea on the terrace."

The girl came – not like Grandmother's Milly, in clogs and a flowery overall, but a girl dressed like a waitress, in a coffee-coloured dress and a white cap and apron – and put a tray with a lace cloth on it down beside Lucy on the parapet of the stone terrace. On the tray were tiny pieces of bread and butter, apricot jam and two home-made fairy cakes, a little silver teapot and thin china with rosebuds painted on it. But Lucy was not hungry. She sat on the terrace thinking about those pale round eyes. She could see the mountains stretching far away, and in front of them the fields and lanes and winding cart roads and the dead blue empty sky. "I am the Princess of Cleves," she told the mountains. It did no good. She is a witch, she thought. And she hates me.

Mabel Twentyman, however, didn't even bother to look in Lucy's direction when it was time for them to go. She looked away over her head instead in a funny sort of way.

"Now you'll be coming down to see us, Mabel," the Missis said. "You're welcome all ways over, you know that." But all Mabel said, fingering her pearls, was: "Ye'll lose a beast in the mire. Think on. And put the child to bed and draw the curtains to." And again Lucy felt the dreadful shiver.

The Missis seemed upset, as well. She tutted and she fretted all the way home on the bus. "Beast in the mire? Beast in the mire? There is no mire this weather. We've lost no beast in the mire. All our cows is standing in the Rough Ground. There's none straying this weather."

"There's a mire in the Sappy Moss," said Lucy, rousing herself. "Milly says it's never dry in the Sappy Moss. It's bottomless bog, Milly says."

"Yes, but there's never any cattle int' Sappy Moss. Oh dearie me – and Mabel's never wrong."

As she left the bus at Blencogo village end and began to walk towards the Rough Ground for home, they saw a little crowd gathered. The three little Hodgson girls were hanging over their garden wall; the Pearson children were all over the road; wild Tom Watson was waving a stick. The whole village seemed to be out. And there in the middle came Lucy's father and her uncle and some other men leading a cow; and the cow was up to its shoulders in dark green, slimy wet mud. "You've nearly lost yon beast int' mire, Missis," people shouted. "It's been strayed int' Sappy Moss. They've been striving for it two hours."

"Well ivvever! Land sakes! Lorgan-days!" said the Missis and not only she but everybody else – in Bromfield Village, Waverton, Blencogo, Aspatria and all the way to Whitehaven, northwards into Abbey Town and south-wards to Mealsgate and Ireby and Caldbeck. By Christmas it had got to Penruddock and Matterdale, Grasmere and Coniston and Boot.

"She told me – just as we was leaving, didn't she Lucy? 'Ye'll lose a beast in the mire,' she said. Well ivvever!" It was a long time since the Missis had been so excited.

Unfortunately, though, she forgot the other thing that the witch had said, and if she hadn't – there's no knowing – Lucy might not have been quite so ill with the measles which she started with a vengeance the very next day.

7

Zoroaster

"'The magus Zoroaster,'" said Lucy,
"'my dead child,
Met his own image walking in the garden'."

"I don't know what you're talking about," said Avice
Mew.

Lucy, Avice Mew and Mary Fell had got up early to
see the sunrise. None of them had seen it before and it
seemed to Lucy time that they did. "After all," she said,
"it can't take long. You often wake up and it's dark and
then you just turn over and it's gone grey, which means
it's over. I'm sure I've often only just missed it." (She
had read in a church magazine of her mother's that if the
dawn only happened once a year everyone in the country
would be up to look at it, it was so marvellous.) "It
comes up from behind the hills but you can't see it from
our house because of Dennis."

"I think I may have seen it once," said Mary Fell. "It
was behind our chimney-pots. But I had tonsillitis."

Avice Mew said nothing. She had never seen the
dawn, nor thought much about it, and she wasn't as it
happened thinking a great deal about it now. It had
taken Lucy and Mary a long time and some sharp words
with Mrs. Mew before Avice could be got out at all at
four o'clock in the morning. They had had to sit on the

Mews' gate-post tops, shouting, for quite a quarter of an hour.

Avice was rather new to the town – well, not born there – and her mother was smart and played Bridge. They had come from the south of England, and nobody knew how to talk to them. "A cut above," said Lucy's Auntie Gladys, "or they think they are." "I'm afraid they are not," said Lucy's mother sadly. "They have paper dinner-napkins."

Avice was very, very pretty. Lucy and Mary had walked round her a bit at first, but she seemed to be vaguely all right, though different, and after a while she seemed to be walking home from school with them each day, though she never said much. She was terribly keen on horses and mad about clothes. Lucy and Mary who were rather younger anyway, never thought about either; yet here she was waiting with them for the sunrise.

Lucy and Mary Fell had known each other since time began – or at any rate since their very first day at kindergarten. "And this is Mary Fell," the teacher with the pin pricks all over her nose had said; and Lucy and Mary had looked at each other and said to themselves, "Here is something different from me," and were friends for ever.

Mary was a wonderful friend. She never quarrelled, she never judged, she never criticised. She hardly ever laughed but she made everybody else laugh; in fact she could make you absolutely roar. She had a large face like

76

a shield. She looked extremely serious but really she saw the world as a lovely mad sort of place underneath. But she thought things out, absolutely straight – she was very good at maths – and she was intensely truthful. Her schoolmistresses adored her. "*That's* right, dear," they said, and turned with a sigh to Lucy.

And Lucy – Lucy who tired people out, who yearned and squirmed and talked too much and wept and railed and tied her little brother up with ropes and slammed doors and packed suitcases and left home, and came back again five minutes later because she had forgotten a book; who worshipped people and loathed people and read a lot of poetry and couldn't learn her tables and was probably a bit mad because in her heart – or so she said – she felt she was not Lucy at all but the Princess of Cleves – Lucy Mary knew as thoroughly – more thoroughly – than a sister.

"What shall I *do* with this child?" wailed Lucy's mother. "I don't care to think what will *become* of her," said their stern headmistress. Yet Mary Fell understood her perfectly. They were the two sides of the same penny piece.

Getting Avice moving had taken so long that the three girls arrived in Dennis garden much later than they had intended and the world was already lightening. The long grass was soaking wet, the long windows shadowed and asleep and the colourless trees looked tired out. The orchard at the end of the garden stood sad and secret. Dark clouds dragged overhead and it was trying to rain.

"If you ask me," said Lucy, "it's over."

"It's not exactly dark still," said Mary, "so it may be just coming."

"No. It's over. That's what."

"You needn't look at me. I can't help being a heavy sleeper." Avice Mew stretched herself like a tiger skin on the summerhouse bed made of old boxes and a smelly blanket that had belonged to Mary Fell's dog, Square Leg. The Fells, like Lucy's Aunt Fanny and Auntie Bea, lived in a house that faced the cricket field. In the back of the summerhouse Lucy had once found a pile of old fashion magazines for ladies, full of pictures of young women with belts round their knees and bands round their foreheads and eyebrows that made them look surprised. Avice loved them.

"I don't know what we're doing here anyway," she said, "I don't know why we came." She flicked the pages.

Mary swung very slowly about on the end of a rope tied to the sycamore tree, dolefully like a bell, in her mackintosh cape. Lucy began to climb the sycamore tree, starting with a leap from the summerhouse roof and somehow clutching a dust-sheet to her stomach. She was unusually dressed in her new tweed coat which had been over the hall chair waiting to be put away for winter after shortening. On her head she wore a man's cap, back to front.

"I suppose that is meant to be some sort of fancy-dress." Avice Mew was glinting like a snake this morning. She was wearing a clean white riding mac, neatly belted in, with little gold eyelet holes under the arms to let out the warm air.

"Shush," said Mary, "she's keen on someone with a hat like that."

"Keen! The only person with a hat like that is the old woman on the coal cart."

Lucy tied the dust-sheet like a bag with two knots six feet apart along a strong branch. Then she dropped down into it and hung in a bulge at the bottom. "I wish we had a real hammock," she said, "I wish Auntie Kitty would send me one. I could rather go to sleep now."

"You look like a bag pudding," said Mary Fell.

"'The magus Zoroaster . . .'"

"Oh shut up about the magus Zoroaster," said Avice.

"'My dead child . . .'" There was a long tearing sound and the pudding fell out of the bag on to the grass.

"'Met his own image walking in the garden'," said Lucy. "I think my back's broken."

"You don't even know what it means."

"I do."

"All right then, translate it."

"Well, it's about this magus."

"What's a magus? I said *translate* it."

"It's a great man. This great man, Zoroaster . . ."

"That's magnus," said Mary Fell who wasn't only clever at sums.

"Well magnus can mean great," said Lucy. "It means big."

"But it isn't magnus, it's *magus*."

"Well, anyway it means great or important or something. Anyone can see it does. Magnus or magus it's the same thing."

"I think it means 'wise'," said Mary Fell mildly. "Like the wise men. They were mag*i* so one of them would have been a mag*us*."

"Well, there you are, you see!"

"I don't think we're really anywhere."

"Oh, do shut up. I'm telling you. This great and wise I suppose man, Zoroaster, who was my dead child . . ."

"How can he be a wise man if he's a dead child?" asked Avice.

"Well, he used to be a dead child. I mean he used to be a child before he was a man, and then he died. It's his mother or someone talking after he's dead."

"She must have been pretty old then."

"Well I expect she was. There's no law about mothers not being old. My mother's old. She's always going on about it. She's always saying, 'I've never had to do the ironing sitting down until this summer,' and stuff like that. I bet your mother is, too."

"My mother doesn't do any ironing," said Mary Fell. "She often forgets to do the washing, too."

"We have someone in to do our ironing," said Avice Mew with a proud look.

"THIS IMPORTANT, WISE MAN ZOROASTER," said Lucy, glaring, "who was my child, once met himself when he was walking in the garden."

"*Met* himself?" said Avice Mew.

"No, wet himself," said Mary Fell. Avice began to shriek and roll about.

"Met himself. Shut up. Met himself. Saw himself coming towards him."

"Oh," said Mary Fell.

"He must have told his mother about it then?"

"Well, of course he did. So would you if you saw yourself coming towards you in the garden."

"I wouldn't," said Avice. "I'd know I was bonkers. Or looking in a pond."

"You mean he actually saw *himself*?" said Mary Fell. "He actually *saw* *himself*, and then he died?"

"Yes," said Lucy, suddenly bored, "he saw himself and told his mother. 'Mother,' he said, 'guess who I saw when I was out in the garden this morning? Myself.' And *she* said, 'What, another of you?' and *he* said, 'Yes,' and *she* said, 'What an 'orrible thought!'"

"No," said Avice. "She said, 'And what were you doing in the garden without your dressing-gown I'll bet?' and *he* said 'I was gazing and gazing at the beeeootiful sunrise.' I'm fed up with this. I'm going home to bed." And she got

81

up and stretched and went off with a bundle of the magazines under each arm.

"He met himself," said Mary Fell without looking up. "He met himself and then he told his mother, and then he died?"

"Perhaps it would have been all right if he hadn't told his mother," called Avice, disappearing through the trellis.

"It'd be like seeing yourself in shop windows," said Lucy. "You do want to die . . . You think, 'Who's that awful . . .'"

"No," said Mary Fell, still very seriously. "No. It means that this man was seeing his soul . . .

"It is a terrible poem," she said in the end. "It is a good thing it's rubbish."

"Why is it rubbish?"

"Because it doesn't happen."

"What doesn't happen?"

"That sort of thing. That sort of magic and stuff."

"How d'you know?"

"Because it must be rubbish if you think. Omens and magic and stuff."

"I don't see . . ." said Lucy. "I don't see," she said.

She went wandering off in her back-to-front hat over the bumpy lawn, swishing at it with a stick. "I don't see . . ." she said. She drew near the sad orchard and plunged in among the trees. There was still very little light. The rain had stopped and a wind had begun to blow. The apple trees tossed noisily above her, flinging their hair. Her legs were cold and soaking in the long grass and getting scratched from gooseberry prickles. She kicked and swished and felt very depressed. "I'm fed up with this," she said. "I don't see anything in it. Sunrise! I shan't bother again."

And then she looked up and saw something absolutely dreadful. It was caught in the branches of an apple tree. It was so dreadful that she had to ignore it. She turned away and went on swishing with a stick. She moved a little way off, keeping her back to it, then she moved further and more quickly; then at last burst on to the lawn and ran wildly back to the place outside the summerhouse where Mary still sat upon her stone.

"I've seen something," she said.

"What?"

"Something awful in the orchard."

"What was it? Yourself?"

"No – bones."

"*Bones*!"

"Yes. A skull. It's up a tree."

"Don't be silly. We'd have seen it before."

They went back and searched, Lucy keeping rather to the edge of the orchard, Mary looking carefully further in, but they could not see any bones.

"You imagined it."

"I did not."

"You did. It would be all that talk about Zoroaster and dying and seeing things."

"I DID NOT," Lucy grew red and began to breathe hard. "I DID NOT IMAGINE IT. I saw it. It was bones. It was a face looking at me."

Mary turned her eyes upon Lucy. She looked disappointed, dreadfully sad.

"You don't believe me, do you?"

Mary picked up the very tip of a gooseberry branch and lifted it to see if there were any fruit hanging underneath.

"You think I'm trying to show you there's omens and magic and stuff and telling lies to prove it. Don't you? That's what you think, don't you? I'm telling you there is a skull up one of the apple trees. I dare say it's just a dog's or an eagle's or something, but it's there and it's awful."

"I didn't see it."

"Well I did."

"Well, where is it then?"

"I don't know." She began to cry. "I'm going home. I'm fed up. I hate you."

That day was the last day of the summer term. After breakfast Lucy and Mary and Avice and everyone went to school for prayers and reports and cloakroom-clearing and shaking hands with Mrs. Stebbing and three cheers for the cook and so on. Then all was over and nine glorious, school-less weeks began. Usually – in fact always – Lucy and Mary went home together on this day, swinging their shoe-bags against railings, flapping their report-envelopes about, singing a little, pushing each other off the pavement, perhaps looking in at Dennis on the way.

Today they did not. Mary walked home with Pamela Simpson. Lucy hung about for Avice Mew, who was combing and combing her orange hair and still looking very sour and tired, and then tramped off on her own.

The next day her father's school broke up and her mother packed for Thornby End – an immense pack-up for the whole of the nine weeks and only bits and pieces for lunch. Usually – in fact always – Mary Fell came round in the afternoon and they messed about and took their books back to the library and bought a lot of comics and were happy. Today Mary did not come. They passed her house on their way to the station in the taxi next morning. Always Mary was at the bathroom window, waving. But not today. All the blinds were drawn. She was obviously sleeping late.

And even Thornby End went wrong that year, because this was the summer when Lucy met the witch and caught the measles and her beautiful grandmother who was perfect in every way, suddenly turned out to be very odd about illnesses. They made her cross, rather than kind like most people, and she kept tappitting about saying, "Tut, tut, tut. I can't abide a room with a sick person in't." The doctor was huge and red and said she must be wrapped in scarlet flannel. The weather was terribly hot. She looked through the brass bars of the bed and said, "I want to see the mountains," but they pulled the blind down and said she would hurt her eyes. But the blind was bright yellow and hurt her eyes just as much; so they hung blankets over it, and she grew hotter and hotter.

Across the ceiling walked a great man made of cracks, a man with a terrible long head. When she was little Lucy had called him "the finger man" – he had long, wavering arms like a daddy-long-legs – but now she called him "Zoroaster". His face was turned from her. "I don't want to see his face," she kept yelling, and her grandfather who was a difficult enough man to begin with thought she meant him and went grumbling and slamming downstairs, roaring at the sheepdogs. "Tut, tut, tut," went her beautiful grandmother, "I can't abide sickness in a house."

Lucy's mother sat beside her a lot of the day, when she wasn't looking after Jake, and her father in the evening when he was no longer wanted in the harvest field. "What's all this about Zoroaster?" he asked. "She keeps going on and on about the zoroasters in Dennis garden." "I expect it's some sort of flower," said her mother. "Well, she doesn't seem to think much of it," her father said.

But Lucy got better at last and sat up and ate brown eggs and laughed with her grandmother and Milly, her grandmother's girl, about all kinds of things again. She sat up in bed in a lace shawl under the best heavy cotton quilt and looked out at Skidder mountain and read the comics she had brought with her; and a great many people came to see her and sank down into a valley at the end of the feather bed, their kind faces beaming, and saying, "The poor little sowl." And they gave her red apples.

"Yer ought till 'ave 'ad yon Mary Fell ower to stay, like last year," said Milly one afternoon. "She'd mek yer laugh like."

Milly was cleaning the kitchen stone before the fire with a lump of chalk, and it was Lucy's first day out of bed. Outside, the tremendous summer had ended in a deluge. The fawn mountains had turned blue and green again overnight, cracked and plumed with the white water of the becks. It was cool and there was a fire in the grate with huge branches sticking four feet out into the room, and earwigs dashing about on them wondering which way to jump. Milly drew a pattern of long figure-of-eights three times upon the stone with the chalk – a pattern people had probably been drawing on stones since the Celts lived in Cumberland.

"She was a funny one, that Mary Fell."

"She doesn't want to come, I expect."

"And whyever?"

"She's gone off me. And anyway you ate all her chocolate last year out of the dressing-table drawer."

"Well she nivver offered it. All that chocolate!" said Milly unashamed.

87

"It was stealing."

Milly began to wash her feet in the washing-up bowl. When they were clean she washed her hands and then her face and dried them all on a frightful bit of towel hanging behind the yard door. She had a lovely complexion and bright green eyes.

"She'll have no luck if she don't share out," she said.

"She doesn't believe in luck. And she doesn't believe in magic," said Lucy.

"Then she'd best tek care," said Milly, throwing her washing water into the yard where it mingled with the rain.

They left the farm on a lovely, ordinary September day, brown and gold with frost in the air and the leaves flying, and the noise of the lively sea to be heard the minute they got down on their own station platform. "Home," said Lucy's mother, "and this time I must say I'm not sorry. Oh Lucy, look, there's Mary Fell."

Mary's chin was resting on the barrier gate and her large face above it looked watchful and excited. She began to wave her arms about as Lucy drew near.

"Hullo," said Lucy.

"Hullo," said Mary with a queer look.

"Has anything happened? I've had the measles."

"Yes. Avice has joined the Girl Guides."

"*Avice* has!"

"Yes, she says the uniform's heaven."

They began to laugh. That is to say they began to snort and howl and gulp and push each other against the ticket collector who dropped the tickets and said, "Now then, NOW THEN!"

"Come on curs, vandals, miserable hounds," called Lucy's father. (He was very happy. He was back to school tomorrow.) "2A + 2A, Mary Fell?" She gave the right answer.

"There's something else," she said to Lucy as they crammed into the taxi. "There's something else. Just you wait. It's something . . ."

As they rounded the corner of the cricket field, there was Dennis, with smoke in the chimneys, the windows sparkling clean and the great double gates painted bright orange.

"It's sold!"

"Good heavens! Never! Sold! It can't be!" cried everyone. "Oh dear, oh dear!" said Lucy's father. "No more compost, no more pea sticks!"

"No more apples or gooseberries or bramble jelly," said her mother. "Now I wonder who on earth . . ."

In the hustle of unpacking and unloading themselves Lucy and Mary made off. Lucy made straight for Dennis by the narrow door in the side wall. Usually – in fact always – she and Mary did this the very minute they reached home but today, though Lucy's step was firm, it was rather desperate. She felt a great weight of sorrow upon her, anger and sadness and the end of the measles heaped upon her heart. For Dennis was gone. It was hers no more.

"We shouldn't be here now," said Mary.

"I don't care."

"We can't just go in as usual. It's not ours any more."

Lucy strode on. They edged round the greenhouses, the kitchen garden, into the currant bushes, until they could see the trellis leading on to the lawns and the orchard. There was no one about.

"We ought to go back now." Mary's voice was no longer magus-like. It was trembly. But she followed on, and Lucy opened the door in the trellis and walked on to the lawn. In front of them was the orchard and standing in the orchard, very near to them, was a thin figure in a long fur coat. Its face was turned away from them under an apple tree and it was examining something in its hands. It was a very tall and quiet figure.

"Oh Lucy! I want to go. I don't want to see its face." Mary's own large face had turned very white. "Lucy, what if it's ourselves?"

"Don't be silly," said Lucy, suddenly strong. "It can't be both of us."

And it wasn't. When it heard them it turned round, and it had the perfectly ordinary face of a nice sort of oldish woman with bright eyes.

"Now then you two girls," it said. "Come here and look at these beautiful bones."

8

One of Jinnie Love's Fair Days

It was the last day of Mrs. Binge-Benson's visit and Lucy's mother wanted to give her a small farewell present.

"*You* want to give *her* . . ." said Lucy's father. "A bit upside down." But Lucy's mother said, "We were Girls Together."

"Like Mary Fell and I?" asked Lucy.

"Oh, well no. You see Mrs. Binge-Benson and I were in different walks of life."

"Walks of fiddle," said Lucy's father.

"What is that?" asked Lucy.

"Well, Mrs. Binge-Benson – Eleanor Holmes as she was then – lived at The Hall and we only lived in a little house in Newcomen Terrace. Sometimes they asked me to tea but our parents didn't call."

"What's 'call'?"

"Well – 'call'. Visit each other."

"Why not?"

"Well – oh Lucy!"

"Didn't they like each other?"

"They just didn't know each other. The Holmeses went everywhere with a trap."

"For mice?"

"No – a trap. A carriage on wheels with brass lamps and a little dappled horse to pull it."

"Well, why couldn't they call in that?" asked Lucy. "You'd think it would make it easier. Anyway I thought you said your family was frightfully grand. We're terribly old – you're always telling us."

"Adam and Eve," said her father.

"Well so it is." Lucy's mother drew herself up. "Very very old. But we fell on hard times. We gave up our lands for the Faith. Henry VIII. Pilgrimage of Grace, 1536. Two of your ancestors were beheaded, Lucy, and one had a piece of his flesh nailed to the church door."

"I know," said Lucy, "but what happened better to the Holmeses and the Binge-Bensons?"

"They were cleverer," said her father.

"I really don't know if there *were* any," said her mother rather grandly.

"Those were the days," said Lucy's father.

"Hush, William! All I say is that Eleanor and I were Girls Together and I shall never forget the lovely times we had. The Hall was wonderful. There now! I don't care what you say. There was a sunken garden and a nannie and a nursery maid to fold the clothes."

"Fold the clothes?"

"Yes, all the children's clothes as they took them off for their baths."

"Goodness, what a funny job!"

"It was very kind of them to ask me to tea. I wish there was someone at The Hall now to ask Lucy to tea. She has been nowhere, seen nothing."

"I don't suppose she wants to see somebody folding clothes," said her father.

"We had such lovely walks." Lucy's mother looked far into the distance. "On the promenade, Lucy, in a procession. There were two dear little boys, like rosebuds, in one of those old basket-work prams, and two or three of Eleanor's little sisters bowling their hoops and a nursery maid with long streamers down her back."

"Folding her wings," said Lucy's father.

"Eleanor and I used to walk along behind, hand in hand. We had fat plaits of hair. And gaiters. Brown shiny gaiters with hundreds of little buttons you had to do up with a button hook. Oh, they were such happy days!"

"It sounds awful," said Lucy rudely.

Her mother shut her eyes. "ALL THAT I AM SAYING," she declared, "is that I want Lucy to go out before Eleanor goes and buy her one of Jinnie Love's Fair Days."

"Well, nobody is stopping you, my love," said Lucy's father. "Goodbye, I'm off to school. I bet she squashes it."

"Eleanor couldn't squash a feather," said Lucy's mother. "Eleanor dear – there you are. I do hope your breakfast was all right?"

Mrs. Binge-Benson came exhaustedly into the room, folded herself into a chair and lay back.

"Delicious," she whispered faintly.

She was a very thin, narrow woman with sloping shoulders and from her head to her feet she was fawn –

fawn hair, fawn face, fawn eyes, fawn cardigan and skirt, fawn lace blouse, fawn brooch, fawn rings, fawn stockings, fawn shoes, and when she smiled, fawn teeth. In her fawn ears were the most wonderful round and softly gleaming fawn pearls which Lucy longed for for her mother. Her fawn feet were as narrow as the heads of two lizards and she had neither eyebrows nor lashes. She really was the most extraordinary-looking person but to Lucy's astonishment all her mother's friends went on about her as if she were a film star. "Beautiful bones," they said, and, "You can always tell."

"Delicious," said Mrs. Binge-Benson again, shutting her eyelids. "I'm afraid I couldn't quite manage the grapefruit – just a tiny bit acid you know. And so sweet of you to send up an egg. I really should have said 'don't' but I thought you remembered. I think it's just the *idea* of an egg . . . in the early morning, don't you think? The runniness, is it? No, I think the *stickiness*. I'm one of these unfortunate people who are sensitive to stickiness." She shuddered and flicked her long fingers about like a pianist at full stretch scattering raindrops. "The coffee," she opened her eyes with a kind smile, "– was delicious."

"Oh I'm so glad," said Lucy's mother beaming.

"Tell me, dear, do you never use *beans*? I must send you some beans from my heavenly coffee man in London. You'll feel you have never tasted coffee before."

"Thank you," said Lucy's mother sadly.

"She's ghastly." Lucy and Mary Fell were off to Jinnie Love's for a cake, for that is what one of Jinnie Love's Fair Days was – a cake. A beautifully light sponge cake with a particularly feathery, sugary filling. Jinnie had been famous for them for many years and they had always been called her Fair Days because when you said, "Good morning Jinnie. May I have a sponge cake? How are you today?" she always answered, "Well, I'm afraid that this is just one of my *fair* days."

Jinnie Love lived in one of the long line of fishermen's cottages. They were such low cottages that they seemed more like rabbit holes than houses. The doors were so low that you had to lean down to rap the knocker and when the door opened there were two steps leading even further down inside and then a long, sandy-coloured passage. To the side of the door was a very clean window with its chin on the pavement, and lace curtains looped stiffly back inside and on a little table between them two or three cakes displayed on frilly doilies.

"Please Miss Love, can Mother have a sponge cake?" asked Lucy.

"That's right. Come along." Jinnie tottered off ahead of them. She was as frail as a cobweb but like cobwebs she seemed able to last for a good long time. Lucy's mother said that she had looked exactly the same when she and Eleanor were Girls Together.

"How are you today?" asked Mary, just to test things out.

"Well my dears, I'm afraid that this is just one of my *fair* days." She wrapped the cake, still on its doily, in a white cardboard box and tied it up with blue string. "Don't eat it on the way home now. That'll be one shilling."

When they were in the street again Mary said, "When does she go?"

"Who? Mrs. Binge-Benson? After lunch. They've gone out this morning to see the Miss Halls where they went to school. They'll be hours."

"Well, we needn't go back straight away then?"

"No, not really."

They both looked across the road at the thin old stile that led on to the sandhills.

"Didn't you once get in a row for going on the sandhills?"

"Oh years ago," said Lucy. "They told me to go away because I was being a nuisance in the kitchen, and I thought they meant I could, so I went off for the day just about, to West Hartlepool or somewhere. I was all alone. There was an awful do."

"They wouldn't mind now. And we're older."

"They did let us watch the sunrise by ourselves. Let's just go for a quick play. We could look for the ship in the grass or something."

"Ha ha."

"I wish we had a watch though." Lucy hung back. "I'm not getting one till my next birthday. If I ever do.

They keep forgetting. Still we can always hear the church I suppose. Oh come on!"

Hair flying, cake box swinging, they were off. "Upwards and onwards," cried Mary, arms afling, as she reached the heights and saw the sea far away across the white sands.

"Chaaaaaaaaaaaarge!" yelled Lucy. They landed over their ankles in soft cold sand that began to flow in silent avalanches down the slopes. They ran through the pale spiky grass, in and out, up and down, and flopped in a cave of sand, its roof coiling over them like a wave. Lucy lay down flat on her back and balanced the cake box on her stomach, very dignified. "I am the Princess of Cleves," she said. "Off with my head. What do I care. . . ."

"I love these cakes," she went on, looking at the box in a friendly way. "Let's have a lick."

"I think she'd notice."

"I just bet she'd notice. 'I really ought to have *told* you – I'm so over-*sensitive* to licked cakes.' Blah."

"Let's blow on it like the Mayor of Toytown."

"'My *deeear*! I simply can't bear *blown* cakes. Now my heavenly little cake man in London never blows on the cakes,' blah and blah and blah."

"Let's poison it," said Mary Fell suddenly.

Lucy rolled her eyes round and looked at her.

"What with?"

"Seaweed."

"How d'you know that's poison?"

"I read it."

"Don't be silly, they make medicine out of it. Iodine."

"Well, that's poison – to swallow."

"Or it might be castor oil."

"A castor oil cake," said Mary Fell. "Hmmmm."

They wandered down towards the sea, over the wavy ribs of sand, pressing their feet into the ridges. "Like the roof of a mouth," said Mary. "Watch out you don't drop the box. 'May deeear! A roof of the mouth cake.'"

"Oh blah – look there's some seaweed."

A great slithery oily-green and toffee-coloured heap of seaweed lay near the edge of the waves. Wet, rich, polished seaweed, nicely coiled. It seemed to be coiled round something and there was a smell of dead fish about and rather a lot of flies.

"Let's put the cake box on it – just to give it a whiff."

"Let's take it *out* of the cake box and put it on the seaweed," said Lucy in a rush of wickedness. "Naked."

They undid the Fair Day and sat it without even its doily on top of the heap. It looked very pretty in the sunshine – round and crumby and buttery yellow.

"Oh Binge! Oh Benson, behold thy cake!" Lucy commanded in a regal voice.

"And may it make thy stomick ache," added Mary Fell.

They found this very funny. Lucy found it so funny that she began to shriek.

"Behold thy cake Binge-Benson do.

"I hope it tastes like mouldy stew." She rolled about on the sands making a tremendous noise and sending the seagulls flying. Mary began to look quite anxious. "Lucy, hush for goodness sake! You sound like a horse or something." Lucy hushed.

"What did you do when you came over the sands by yourself before – all that time ago?" Mary asked, just for something to say. Lucy sat up and looked out to sea at the great ships sliding past towards the docks, and the cream and rosy clouds above the chimneys of the steel works. "Oh shut up," she said.

"All right! What's the matter now? I only said . . ."

"Shut up. Come on. I'm going home," and Lucy got up with a very sour expression on her face, fell over her own feet, flung out her arms to save herself and put her fist right through the middle of Jinnie Love's Fair Day.

A great silence fell upon the beach.

"Oh help!" she said. "Whatever shall we do?"

They peered into the hollow in the middle of the mound and what was left of the cake could be seen within, mixed up with sand and excited-looking flies. "There's an awful smell of fish. I think it's a dead jelly-fish."

"Do you think we could save just the bottom layer or something?"

"Well I think we ought to try." Mary looked very grave. Unhopefully they began to scoop what they could back into the box.

"It looks so awful that . . . I don't think I've ever seen anything so awful."

"I don't think I *can* look," said Mary, turning her eyes unto the hills.

Lucy did up the box again with the blue string and they slowly started for home and neither of them spoke until they got to the stile. Then Mary stood still.

"We're cracked," she said. "It's easy."

"What's easy?"

"Have you got a shilling?"

"Yes – I've got my pocket money."

"Well then – it's easy."

"What?"

"GO AND BUY ANOTHER."

"Another Fair Day?"

"Yes."

"With my pocket money?"

"Yes."

"Oh well yes – I suppose I could. It's an awful lot."

"Well what'll you do? You can't give her that one."

"I *suppose* not." Lucy's eyes began to gleam.

"No you can not," said Mary, "YOU CAN NOT. Go on – leave the box here and go and get another one. There was another in the window."

Five minutes later they were on their way once more,

walking briskly through the churchyard and nearly home.

"What did she say?"

"She said, 'So you did eat it on the way home. I thought as much. Just as well you had another shilling.'"

"Well it was just as well . . . I say . . ."

"What?"

"What shall we do with the other one? The seaweed one?"

"Oh I don't know. Dump it down somewhere. Let's put it on a grave."

"No. Not on a grave. I don't know."

"We could take it back and throw it away on the sandhills."

"There isn't time. Look at the clock."

"Oh help, and they're sure to see us coming in with it. Let's just . . ." Lucy looked round, "let's just leave it in church."

"Wouldn't someone mind?"

"I don't see why. Mother's always saying, 'Take your sins to church.'"

"I wouldn't say the cake was a sin exactly."

"Well it might have been a sin if we hadn't had another shilling."

"Just having money doesn't make any difference. You can't just pay and get rid of sins."

"Oh, I don't know. I *needn't* have bought another. It

means I can't buy anything else for over a week. I bothered to put it right. My sin's washed out."

"But if you'd had no money?"

They thought about this. "Well, whether it's a sin or not what's in the box isn't a sin," said Mary.

"I don't know what you're talking about."

"Well a cake – just a cake, made of butter and stuff, can't be a sin. It's not what's in the box that's a sin – it's what we did to what's in the box – I mean what you did to it."

"I – we did plenty to it."

"Yes, but the sin wasn't something you can get hold of, like what's in the box. You can't call a *cake* a sin. I can see you could leave a sin in church but you can't go leaving cakes."

"Well, would you call it a trouble then? Mother says 'Leave all your sins and *troubles* in church.'"

"I suppose so. Yes, it's a trouble all right."

"'Leave all your sins and troubles. Offer them,' she says. So we'll offer the cake."

"All right, I suppose so then."

They pushed open the heavy door and walked up the centre aisle to the chancel. No one was there. Sunshine with dust in it shone through the coloured glass. Silver candlesticks on the altar gleamed darkly.

"D'you feel you're being watched, Lucy?"

"Always. It always feels full of people except in services." She went up and undid the brass rail before the altar. Then she firmly placed the cake box on the altar beneath the cross. She stepped back, bowed, closed the altar rail and joined Mary again. They waited a moment and then Mary said, "I suppose we'd better be going."

At two o'clock precisely Mrs. Binge-Benson's beautiful fawn car was at the gate with its chauffeur holding the door. Her luggage was packed out of sight, a fur rug (fawn) was ready on the seat for her knees and she was turning to say goodbye. She gave Lucy and Mary her fingertips to touch for a moment, gently placed her hand on Jake's head, which jerked away, gave Lucy's father a tired smile and, leaning forward, put her cheek against Lucy's mother's cheek and kissed the air. "My *dear* – such a lovely time. So heavenly to remember all those ancient days. And the Miss Halls still alive – simply amazing! And you darling – and your dear little house and your nice little family . . ." (Lucy's father turned his back and gave a great trumpet-call into his handkerchief.) "You *must*, you simply must come and see me one of these days in Kensington. You *need* it, dear. It would be so thrilling for you."

"And a present!" she added. "My dear! My dear, it's not? NOT one of Jinnie Thingummy's Fair Days? Oh how marvellous! No, I won't open it now. I'll keep it to *gloat* over at Sheffield Terrace. Darling, you are *brilliant* – I've been telling everyone for years about these marvellous cakes."

"Goodbye," she called faintly, avoiding Jake's swinging foot as she melted into the car, "Goodbye," long fingers drooping from the window, cake box balanced on her knees – and she was gone.

"Goodbye," said Lucy's mother flatly. "Oh well."

"Oh must you pick your *nose*, Jake," she cried suddenly and went dashing into the house with a very dismal and hopeless face.

"Goodbye, goodbye, stinker-poo," sang Jake.

"That'll do," said his father. "Come along for a walk and give your mother a rest."

"Can Mary and I come with you?"

"Yes, if you like. We'll take Jake for a play in the churchyard."

"Oh well – no – thank you. I think we'll stay here, shall we, Mary?"

"And for why because?"

"We've been in the churchyard today."

On the road south Mrs Binge-Benson leaned back against the fawn car cushions. "So," she said, then closed her eyes and sighed. After a minute she opened her eyes and looked at the cake box. "What a strange smell of fish," said she.

9

Jake's Queed

On a sunny and beautiful day in May when the white North Sea was tipped rose pink in the morning sun and the Cleveland Hills looked blue and gentle, Lucy was lying on the floor of the dusty attic in the old empty house, Dennis, trying to get hold of her outstretched toes and roll about in a ring like a whiting.

"I'm an akkerbeest," she said to Mary Fell.

Mary was balancing on her stomach over the dormer window-ledge. "What's a nakkerbeest? It makes a change."

"Why does it make a change?"

"From the Princess of Cleves. I'm a polycarp!"

"An akkerbeest has eyes of flame. It's a big soft lizard. It rolls on the floors of empty houses. Rolling and rolling, heavy and soft. Rolling in the sun. Horrible."

"And singing," she added.

"I'm a polycarp," said Mary Fell.

"Singing in Latin."

"Polycarps have red fangs. They lie out over window-ledges like gargoyles going to be sick. Oh –"

"Better be careful." The akkerbeest undid itself. "I saw your soles."

"Polycarps haven't got souls." The polycarp dropped down into the room. "There's some people in the garden."

"Don't be silly." Lucy heaved herself up to the ledge and looked down at the bumpy grass – more of a meadow than a lawn – and down the summerhouse chimney. The garden slept in the sunshine. "It'll just be Phyllis to say to go for dinner. Oh help, where's Jake?"

"In the turret probably. There *were* some people."

Across the landing there was another large attic with a little door across the corner leading into a dark place like an upside-down ice-cream cornet. In the shadows of this place sat Jake, surrounded by his private belongings and his bed of hay. He had a candle in a bottle and was holding a matchbox.

"I'm an AKKERBEEST," pounced his sister.

"I'm a POLYCARP."

Jake raised his five-year-old eyes and said, "Go 'way. I'm a queed."

"Oh shut up. It's dinner-time," said Lucy pulling.

"You mustn't ever have matches," said Mary Fell. They tugged and scuffled and Jake kicked and yelled, "Go 'way. It's my queed."

Lucy got the box in the end and opened it but it was empty.

"Nothing in it silly, soppy, poggit."

Jake began to cry. "It's my queed. It's my queed. You let it out." And he started roaring and flinging himself about in the hay and the dusty ribs of plaster on the floor.

"Hush!"

Lucy was so stern that he did.

"Hush!"

They all sat absolutely still in the dark, listening. Far down below them there was the great slam of the front door and the booming of feet and then a high voice talking.

"It *was* people!"

"I told you it was."

"Whatever are they doing? They're in the *house!*"

"Perhaps they're going to buy it."

"Don't be silly. Quick!"

With a great heave Lucy seized Jake round his waist where he hung with his face pressed into her stomach. "Quick. Back stairs and kitchen garden," and they set off down to the next landing, round a corner, down again into the corkscrew of the servants' staircase and there they stood, quite still, as the noise of feet and calling voices grew nearer and nearer and nearer.

"Oh heavens!" Lucy looked at Mary and Mary looked at Lucy and Jake looked at the pattern on the front of Lucy's dress. His face was like thunder still but he didn't make a sound.

Nobody knew quite why the house was called "Dennis". Some people said it was the name of the builder's son, though in that case, why hadn't anybody thought of changing it? "Some quite nice people used to live there when your grandmother was a girl," Lucy's mother had said.

"Perhaps they liked it being called Dennis."

"Oh, Lucy, how could they!"

"Perhaps it was the name of a dog or a cat they had."

"Or a goldfish," said Jake.

"You don't call houses after goldfish."

"When I was a girl," said their mother, "I used to go to lovely Guy Fawkes parties there. We had supper at a long, long table in the dining-room and then we all gathered round the windows to watch the bonfire being lit. *They* didn't seem to mind the name. But I think they were dentists."

"Are dentists called Dennis?"

"Oh yes – often I think."

Except for a few months when Lucy was younger the house had been empty for years and years and years. Houses did stand empty in those days, especially great ugly ones like Dennis. The few months when it had been lived in had been exciting though, for a strange woman wrapped in furs had arrived with a group of Indian servants. One of them in a dirty turban had painted the great double gates orange. Van-loads of ivory and carved wooden figures, painted furniture, ostrich plumes, tall metal storks standing on one leg, gilded mirrors, brass gongs and mother-of-pearl screens had been carried in. Great fires had been lit and a grand cleansing of rooms had taken place. In the night queer music had floated out over the North Sea, eastwards over the cricket field and westwards over the vicarage. The members of the cricket team had looked at one another and the Vicar had raised his eyes from his books and Jinnie Love in her little house on the edge of the sandhills had stopped beating her cakes for a moment, and they had all of them shaken their heads.

The lady in furs had glared at everybody and had never been at home when anyone called. Lucy and Mary Fell had spoken to her, but hardly anybody else. Why she had come nobody knew and where she went to nobody knew – for go she did, within a week or two of the last great load of tiger skins and elephants' foot ashtrays, which were all packed up again and disappeared. All that could be seen of the labels said that the packages were NOT WANTED ON VOYAGE. Lucy saw them go sadly.

But with their departure Dennis was her own again – the great shaggy lawn, the sycamore tree and the summerhouse, the houses she made, rounded like nests in the long grass under the apple trees, the cave under the redcurrant bushes with seats made of stones like black sponges from the rockery. Auntie Kitty gave her a rope once and someone fastened it to a high branch and she learned to climb to the top, and then climb even higher and stick her head out of the top circle of leaves and swing herself about with the leaves like a collar.

"Oh, I'm sure they're quite safe," said her mother to people, "and really you can't call it trespassing. They do no harm there. There isn't a pond, or an elm tree to drop branches on them. I must admit I do sometimes think of *tramps*, but the tramps one sees are so very fat. I'm sure

113

they could never climb the gates. After all they're just across the road. No – I think dear Dennis is a blessing. A real *blessing*." By "Dennis" she meant of course the garden. It didn't occur to her that there might be any thought of going into the house which as everyone knew was securely locked and barred.

Everybody knew this and so it was just because Lucy was in a dreamy sort of mood one day, sitting on the cracked steps leading up to one of the long dining-room windows, that she put the tips of two fingers under the sash. She was watching woodlice tearing about in their usual fuss to get the day over, and Mary Fell was lying on the grass eating radishes that they had sown earlier that year. Avice Mew who was with them for once – usually on Saturdays she went riding because her parents were rich – was telling them about various horses. They were sitting there and Lucy put her finger tips under the window sash – and up slid the window without a single sound.

And not once had any of them said. Not even Avice Mew. Not even Jake who was still so young. Not even Lucy who told everything that had ever happened and a few things more. They melted into the house from that day forward and they never spoke about it to a soul. They didn't as a matter of fact even talk about it very much to one another. It was odd. "Just going over to Dennis," they said, and glided through the window and disappeared. They stepped through the window into a dry dusty smell and the most curiously peaceful feeling. They

114

wandered in the cellars for dares, peering in the wine bins, and on dry days they got out on to the roof and watched the road in one direction and the hills in the other, but mostly they didn't do anything but wander about and talk, first in one room and then in another. It was warm and clean, with beautiful wallpaper curling a little bit here and there. Dim mirrors beamed out above dutch-tiled mantelpieces, there were porcelain speaking tubes painted with violets, round handbasins with blue flowers drawn inside them and fierce brass taps; lavatories with sweeping wooden seats like the yokes of oxen and stiff bell-handles that set red flickers jumping in a glass case over the door in the really dreadful old kitchen.

They were in paradise. They were quite safe. How do you explain to people that you have broken in to a house not to feel excited but to feel safe? How do you tell this to your mother sewing pillowcases? "It's like paradise," you say, and she says, "Paradise? Dennis? But it's the ugliest house in the world. It's so clumsy. It's so enormous. It's painted blackcurrant-colour over red brick and the blackcurrant is all flaking off. The windows stick out like elbows and there's that awful turret pointing up to that awful weathercock that's not even been made to spin. Dennis paradise! That simply awful kitchen . . ."

"What a simply awful kitchen!"

A high voice came suddenly from very near at hand. Someone had opened the baize door to the back stairs and the booming of feet on wood changed to scraping as they walked across the servants' cement.

"Cold," grumbled a man's voice, very near indeed, "stone floors, for goodness sake!"

"Not damp though," and a shadow floating and greenish and a hat like a harebell turned towards the servants' stairs. Lucy, Mary and Jake melted into a cupboard.

"Cry and I'll kill you," Lucy's eyes said to Jake. The feet went past.

The cupboard was half-way down the stairs, long and low but very light because its other main wall was glass that looked down into the servants' sitting-room. It was like an indoor greenhouse, but it had probably been used for apples or jam jars. There was a nice smell inside it. The glass was dirty but you could see shapes through it and the children crept across and looked down. The harebell hat went by and a tweed cap and a young man's head without a hat but with a mouth that was sucking the knob of a walking stick. Jake stretched his arm out suddenly through one of the small open panes that had been left to allow the apples or jam jars to breathe, and emptied some air out of his fist into the room below, and nobody looked up.

"Oh a calendar!" suddenly cried the harebell hat. "1921 – do look. It must have been the cook's. The King looks quite a boy." "I thought they said *Indians*," said the tweed cap. "Must have got left over from before."

The harebell hat clutched at its throat. "Oh darling!"

116

she cried, "do let's buy it. It's a glorious house. It's so charming. It's Great Uncle Harry all over again. Bimbo – isn't it a scream?"

The hatless one brought the knob of his walking stick out of his mouth with a pop. "No more cooks," he said. "No more kings, I dare say. War coming, what?" They clattered on. Soon the front door boomed again and all was quiet.

Dinner-time was quiet too – or not so much quiet as thoughtful. At last Lucy's mother said, easing herself about ominously in her chair and looking intently at the stewed rhubarb, "Now Lucy, don't get silly, and try to be calm, but – but I think that somebody may be going to buy Dennis."

"Not certain," said her father, drumming his fingers. "Not certain at all."

There was a silence except for Mary Fell, who was staying the day, scraping up the rest of her juice. Nobody looked at anybody, least of all Lucy.

Then Jake suddenly threw his dirty matchbox at her and it fell in the custard and everyone began to shout.

"It's his queed," said Lucy heavily, lifting it out on her fork.

"Queed? Queed?"

"That's what he says. There's nothing in it."

"Not now," said Jake. "It's gone."

"It always was gone."

"No it wasn't, it was in my pocket all the time out of your way. I hate you."

117

Lucy kicked Jake very hard indeed, straight to his shin bone under the table. She heard the bone. He screamed.

"Jake's a liar!" Horror of horrors, even Mary Fell began to cry.

"STOP," Lucy's mother was on her feet, breathing hard. "This is all I can bear! STOP! There are children in Europe at this moment homeless. Homeless! Shot at! Starving! They are HELPLESS! Europe!" she cried, pointing fiercely in the direction she thought it might be, so that for years Lucy could not think of France or Italy without seeing the dining-room clock standing at 1.30. "Europe! You don't know what Europe *is*. You don't know anything. All you can do is talk baby-talk and dangle about on a rope in Dennis garden.

"Not even Girl Guides! You are nothing! Nothing! Not a word of French! Who is the Foreign Secretary?"

"Oh Kathleen, for goodness' sake!" said Lucy's father.

"Who is the Foreign Secretary?"

"I don't know."

Her mother sat down. "There!" she said. "We are on the point of war and she doesn't know the name of the Foreign Secretary. Eleven years old! Here is *The Daily Telegraph*. You are to go to bed till tea-time. Jake?"

"Can take *The Times*," said her father.

"Don't be silly, William. Jake can go and read the Prayer Book. And Mary can go home."

"Oh Mother, NO. She's staying the day."

"It is a punishment," said her mother. "It is in the

hope that you and Mary will both grow slightly less silly. Jake has time. You have not."

But though Mary did go home she was soon back again. At six o'clock she came round with Avice Mew and went up to Lucy's room without being seen, because Lucy's mother was at Evensong and her father was listening to the news on the wireless. They found Lucy flat on her front on the bed with her eyes shut and *The Daily Telegraph* on the floor unopened.

"I've brought you some tea," Mary said, taking bread and butter from her pocket and looking out of the window at Dennis's purple gables. Between its chimney-pots the hills drifted with their lines of crooked trees straining away from the sea.

"It looks nice on the hills," said Mary. "Let's get our bikes out."

"Shall we get our bikes out?" she asked again and Avice stretched herself and yawned like a cat. "I don't want to go back to Dennis, do you?"

Jake came in. "I've brought you a biscuit, Lucy."

"Oh *say* something!" said Mary. Lucy turned her face sideways but did not open her eyes.

"'My name is Ozymandias, King of Kings'," she said.

"Did you find out about the Foreign Secretary?"

"'Look on my works, ye Mighty, and despair!'"

"Oh do shut up – let's go out. Let's go on the hills for a change. We can't go on the sands with all the barbed wire going up and we don't want to go back to Dennis."

"Why don't we want to go?"

"I don't know."

"Oh *Bimbo*!" said Avice Mew suddenly, gazing into the distance. Mary must have told her.

"What a *scream*!" said Mary Fell. "*Charming*!"

"Charming, charming, charming!" sang Jake.

"Charming," suddenly shrieked Lucy, "I'm a charming akkerbeest." She rolled off the bed.

"I'm a charming polycarp."

"You're mad," said Avice, stroking her silky hair.

"I'm a charming akkerbeest, singing in Latin and baring my fangs."

"I'm a charming polycarp that's eaten the cook."

"No more cooks. They're all akkerbeests and polycarps."

"Polycarps and pollywogs."

"Pollywogs and queeds," said Jake. "I dropped my queed on her old hat and it's eaten her up."

"Hurrah!" cried the akkerbeest, getting hold of its feet and rolling in a ring like a whiting. "They won't come back."

"They won't dare," said the polycarp.

"They've gone 'way," said the queed.

And they had. Dennis stayed empty till the soldiers came.

THROUGH THE DOLLS' HOUSE DOOR

Jane Gardam

Claire and Mary love the dolls' house and its curious assortment of residents: the outsize Dutch doll, Miss Bossy; the General and his troop of Trojan soldiers; the miserable Small Cry; the mysterious Sigger ... But little do the girls know of the extraordinary lives and adventures, past and present, of this resourceful band and the marvellous stories they have to tell.

"An original story ... wry and funny, and full of a sharply poignant sense of the passage of time."
Jill Paton Walsh, Books for Keeps